D0284709

The ENCHANTED LIFE of VALENTINA MEJÍA

The ENCHANTED LIFE of VALENTINA MEJÍA

ALEXANDRA ALESSANDRI

atheneum
ATHENEUM BOOKS FOR YOUNG READERS
New York London Toronto Sydney New Delhi

ATHENEUM BOOKS FOR YOUNG READERS
An imprint of Simon & Schuster Children's Publishing Division
1230 Avenue of the Americas, New York, New York 10020
This book is a work of fiction. Any references to historical events, real people, or real places are used fictitiously. Other names, characters, places, and events are products of the author's imagination, and any resemblance to actual events or places or persons, living or dead, is entirely coincidental.

Interior design by Debra Sfetsios-Conover
The text for this book was set in Charlonka.
Manufactured in the United States of America
0123 FFG
First Edition
10 9 8 7 6 5 4 3 2 1
Library of Congress Cataloging-in-Publication Data
Names: Alessandri, Alexandra, author.
Title: The enchanted life of Valentina Mejía / Alexandra Alessandri.
Description: First edition. | New York : Atheneum Books for Young Readers, [2023] | Audience: Ages 8–12. | Audience: Grades 4–6. | Summary: "To save their father's life, a brother and sister must journey across a land full of magical beings from Colombian folklore and find the most powerful and dangerous of them all—the Madremonte"—Provided by publisher.
Identifiers: LCCN 2022004239 (print) | LCCN 2022004240 (ebook) | ISBN 9781665917056 (hardcover) | ISBN 9781665917070 (ebook)
Subjects: CYAC: Folklore—Colombia—Fiction. | Magic—Fiction. | Mythical animals—Fiction. | Families—Fiction. | Colombia—Fiction. | LCGFT: Novels.
Classification: LCC PZ7.1.A4345 En 2023 (print) | LCC PZ7.1.A4345 (ebook) | DDC [Fic]—dc23
LC record available at https://lccn.loc.gov/2022004239
LC ebook record available at https://lccn.loc.gov/2022004240

To my familia, who filled my childhood with stories of Colombia so I'd always remember

ONE

Three hours into their trek through the Andes, Valentina heard it. At first, she was sure it was another coati. The whining of the raccoonlike animal had been following them for a few miles. But now she thought she heard the distinct sound of heavy breathing.

The skin on her arms erupted in goose bumps.

"¿Escuchaste?" Papi whispered.

"Maybe," Valentina said, a little too loudly. "It's probably the wind."

Papi brought a finger to his lips. "You're going to scare it away."

Her brother, Julián, bounced on his heels, his eyes almost black beneath the shade of tall ferns and even taller trees, which blocked out most of the light in this patch of the jungle. They were far from their farm and the slopes cultivated with coffee beans.

Valentina blew out a breath.

She loved her dad's eccentricities. She did. But the last thing she wanted to do on the first day of summer was track down a patasola. According to legends, the one-legged woman wandered through the countryside looking for victims. Usually, men. She lured them with beautiful singing or cries for help, and when they were within reach: *bam!* She caught them and sucked their blood.

Kind of like a vampire, but cooler.

One thing was listening to the stories in the comfort of Papi's study, though, and another was trudging through the Colombian jungle in search of a creature that didn't exist.

"Sí, Vale," her brother said. "Just 'cause you'd rather be drawing your stupid pictures doesn't mean you have to ruin the fun for everyone."

Valentina opened her mouth to retort, but Papi hissed, "Stop it. Both of you. Don't make me regret bringing you."

"This was *your* idea," Valentina mumbled. "I would've much rather stayed home."

Papi frowned. "You know that's not an option. You're twelve—"

"Almost thirteen," Valentina corrected.

"Too young. Now basta. Let's go." He pushed deeper into the trees without waiting for an answer.

Julián stuck his tongue out at her, then bounded after their dad.

It wasn't fair. Papi insisted on treating her like a little kid. It's not like she would've been alone, anyway. Doña Alicia, their housekeeper, would've been there.

Why did Mami have to be called away for work *this* weekend? She had been sent with her team to el Nevado del Ruiz, near Manizales, because the volcano was threatening to erupt again. Mami, who was a geophysicist, was part of a group of scientists who were studying the recent eruptions and earthquakes happening across Colombia, especially since they were getting stronger and occurring more often. Valentina knew Mami's job was important, but she wished she didn't have to be dragged through the jungle, all because Papi didn't trust her to stay home without him.

If you asked *him*, though, the reason he'd brought them was so they could "get to know the magic running in the veins of this country."

As if magic really existed.

Again the heavy breathing came, sending shivers down Valentina's spine.

"Wait!" she called, sprinting after her father and brother. She did *not* want to be left alone with whatever was out there.

As she reached Julián, she pushed back the damp locks that had come loose from her ponytail. Sticky sweat dripped down her face, and her T-shirt clung to her skin. She'd give anything to be in her room, drawing in peace and feeling the sweet, cool breeze drifting through her open window. It was her favorite spot on the whole farm.

She and her brother walked in silence behind Papi as he scouted the area, listening closely for any signs of the imaginary patasola.

Nearby, a bird warbled. Valentina craned her neck until she found it perched on a bare branch a few feet away. She itched to stop and draw its bright red head and yellow beak, which contrasted against its green body. Her gaze shifted to the vines hanging from the branch and to the dried moss clinging to them.

With the hazy light breaking through the treetops, this scene would make a perfect addition to her portfolio, which she'd been building since last year. She thought wistfully of the sketch pad and charcoal pencils tucked in her mochila.

Back home, her finca sat in a valley an hour south of Medellín. From her window, she could see the humps of the Andes, rows of coffee bushes and banana trees, and a smattering of houses from nearby towns. She wasn't allowed past their property's fence, so she'd only been able to draw the main house with Mami's periwinkle hydrangeas, the copse of bamboo surrounding them, the small pond with geese at the center, and Papi's cottage studio beside it. She'd even drawn a few wild parrots.

While her sketches were nice, they were missing something special.

The way she saw it, if she was being forced to come on this trip, she might as well take advantage and make her portfolio stronger. Then maybe, just maybe, it would be good enough for Señora

Ramirez to recommend her for the Bogotá Academy of Arts next year.

And, if Valentina got in, maybe Mami would let her leave their boring finca and go live in the capital with her abuelitos. She could have a normal life, with movies and malls and maybe even sleepovers.

But that was a lot of maybes.

"¡Vamos!" Julián said, tugging her arm. "You're going to make us lose the patasola. Or"—he paused, grinning mischievously—"she might sneak up behind you when you're distracted."

She glared at her brother and followed Papi through the narrow path between trees. Every so often, he paused, placed his palm on the earth, and peered into the bare bushes, as if he were tracking a wild animal. Julián watched their father and mimicked him, which made Valentina shake her head in amusement. They looked ridiculous.

The farther they went, the more her feet crunched on dry leaves littered across the cracked dirt. Everywhere around her, the earth seemed to thirst. Valentina realized the worst drought in Colombia's history had reached this jungle. It had started in the northern tip of the country several years ago, and slowly, like spilled ink spreading across canvas, it had stretched toward their finca and continued south.

To here.

According to Mami, the drought and the increase in earthquakes and eruptions went hand in hand. Mami blamed it on deforestation and pollution, which had gotten worse in recent decades and which, in her words, were "going to destroy our land." There was rarely a night when Mami wasn't ranting about greedy people and the extinction of Colombia's ecosystems.

A familiar uneasiness settled over Valentina as the nightmare from the night before rushed forward. In it, she stood at the edge of her finca, drawing the scenery. Suddenly, the earth trembled so fiercely it knocked her down before bursting open at her feet. Fire sparked and spread across their fields, reaching toward home. Valentina remembered screaming for Julián and her parents, just as volcanoes jutted out from the crevice, shooting lava and boulders from their craters.

The earth is not happy.

Valentina shuddered as the words flashed through her thoughts. She'd been having the nightmares more often recently. The weirdest part was that afterward, her body tingled with an ache so strong, it felt like someone she loved had died. She couldn't explain it, and when she'd made the mistake of mentioning it to Mami, her mother had scoffed. "Your papá's stories are filling your head with cucarachas."

Honestly, Mami and Papi were as different as the sun and the moon. One chased science, the other tracked leyendas. How they got along was beyond her, but they did. They seemed as happy as when they'd first met at the university. She'd even caught them dancing vallenato in the kitchen a few times, when they thought no one was looking.

Maybe Mami and Papi got along *because* they had such different personalities; each one kept the other grounded. Meanwhile, Valentina occupied some space between the two of them—too creative for Mami, too logical for Papi—and she felt like she didn't belong anywhere.

Now, in the jungle, silence descended. No birds warbled. No coatis whined. Even the heavy breathing seemed to vanish.

A twig broke ahead, and Papi froze.

"Did you hear that?" Julián mouthed, his eyes glittering with excitement.

Valentina had, but that could've been any of the wildlife living here. Monkeys. Snakes. Mountain tapirs. Bespectacled bears. Even jaguars might be prowling around. She shuddered at the thought of coming face-to-face with a growling carnivorous cat.

Papi met their gazes and pressed a finger to his lips.

Slowly, he slipped out a net from his mochila. He lowered a pair of heat-vision goggles over his eyes and crept forward, keeping low to the ground.

Beside her, Julián tensed.

Part of Valentina wanted to roll her eyes and huff, *It's just another animal.* But she couldn't keep her heart from pumping faster. Could it be? What if they really *did* catch a patasola? Would the creature look the way Papi described her—one leg, matted hair, sharp fangs? It *would* be cool if the creatures from Papi's stories existed. Kind of like magic becoming real, a break from the boringness of farm life.

She wouldn't say that aloud, though.

Instead, she waited beside her brother beneath the shade of giant robles and watched as her father inched toward the sound, the net clutched in his hands and the goggles making him look like some sort of alien.

Another twig snapped. Then came a shuffle between ferns. Papi crouched even lower. Beads of sweat dripped down his face. His mouth pressed into a thin line. Valentina edged forward, anticipation buzzing in her bones as Julián gripped her arm. Neither of them spoke.

In a single fluid movement, Papi swung the net and a shrill, piercing shriek echoed across the jungle.

TWO

The beast caught within the net thrashed and bucked.

Valentina squinted, confused. It was large, but not as tall as a humanlike mythical being would be. Four strong legs stomped against the dried leaves. Its thick body was covered in brown fur. The more she stared, the more she saw it resembled a baby elephant, only with an elongated head and a shorter trunk, which flailed as it struggled to break free.

Then the creature screeched—loud and piercing. Birds scattered above her, flapping higher into the treetops. The hairs on her arms stood as Valentina pressed her hands against her ears to muffle the sound.

She knew exactly what they'd caught.

"That's not a patasola." Valentina shook off her brother. "That's a mountain tapir." She felt the sting of disappointment much sharper than she wanted to admit, and it made her feel ridiculous.

Papi turned to them, a sheepish smile on his face. "Well, that was a flop." He pushed his goggles up on his head and went to cut the animal free. Valentina huffed.

Papi was something of an expert on legends. He'd gotten his PhD in history, and with Abuelito's encouragement, he became a folclorólogo—someone who studied the history of myths and legends. He taught classes about them at the local university, and he'd even written several books on the subject. He often traveled across the country researching and recording sightings—stories from gullible people who claimed to have seen el mohán, la mano peluda, la patasola, or any other creature. Papi always hoped to catch one, to ask it questions and get "valuable information."

Every single time, he came home empty-handed and deflated.

After the last book he published, *The True and Accurate Account of Colombian Legends*, people started to think he was crazy. Why couldn't he accept these myths for what they were: scary stories people liked to tell to control their kids? Mami blamed Abuelito for filling his head with nonsense, though sometimes she, too, got caught up in the legends' magic.

"That patasola is wicked smart," Julián said. "Talk about a fake-out."

Valentina rolled her eyes. "You're ten. Aren't you too old to believe in all this?"

"Don't complain when she creeps up on you in the middle of the night."

Before she could retort, a sudden rush of queasiness hit her.

The earth is not happy.

Her skin tingled, and she broke out in a cold sweat. The locket hanging from her neck burned. She swayed, bracing herself against the moss-covered trunk of a nearby tree.

Slowly, she reached for her canteen in her mochila and took a swig of the cool water. It helped, but her belly still tightened. She settled on the ground and rummaged in her bag for the empanadas Doña Alicia had packed them, hoping the meat patties would settle her stomach. She found them squished beneath the emergency kit her dad had insisted they pack.

Julián sat beside her and pulled out his own lunch.

Soon, after the mountain tapir finally scampered away with an indignant shriek, Papi joined them. He looked defeated, and Valentina felt a twinge of guilt at her annoyance.

"It's okay," she said, finishing the last of her empanadas. "You'll get it next time."

It was a lie and Papi probably knew it, but he gave her a grateful smile.

"Can you tell us a story?" Julián asked.

As Papi dove into one of his tales woven from the legends he knew so well, Valentina took out her sketchbook and charcoal pencils and started outlining the mossy trees and nearby ferns. A sliver of light broke through and bathed the area in a soft glow.

Her shoulders relaxed. Her heartbeat slowed. The longer she sketched, the more the world around her dissolved. Even the uneasiness and nausea seemed to disappear. It was just her and the landscape around her.

There. She leaned back, staring at the drawing in front of her. Not bad. She erased a few lines and redrew them until she was satisfied.

With a nod, Valentina set down the charcoal. She was about to pick up her colored pencils when she felt it again. That deep rumble in her belly, fierce and hot and painful. She clutched her stomach. Her bones ached. She felt as if someone were crushing her chest.

"Papi," she wheezed. She tossed the sketch pad and charcoal pencil aside and threw up.

"¡Amor!" Her father rushed to her side. "Are you okay?"

Julián wrinkled his nose. "Gross."

Valentina hardly heard them over the thrum in her ears. It was as if she were underwater, the only sound coming from her beating heart.

It's happening.

The thought came from nowhere, but the moment it registered, Valentina jumped up, panic surging through her. She shoved her art supplies into her bag. "We have to get out of here."

Her breath came in short gasps.

"But we just sat down," Julián said.

"What's wrong, amor?" Papi asked.

"Please," she said, almost sobbing.

The pressure kept building. Her chest ached to burst. Her thoughts jumbled. They needed to move. To leave the forest. She glanced wildly around her. The trees were so thick and tall, and she knew—even though she had no idea why—they were in danger here.

"Please, Papi," she repeated. "We need to go."

He frowned but didn't push it. "Okay, then."

Valentina almost sagged with relief. Maybe it was his research on myths and legends, or his belief in the supernatural. She didn't care what made him believe her, only that he did.

Julián grumbled, "Who's the silly one now?" But he didn't argue as Papi led them back up the mountain, toward the edge of the road where their truck was parked.

The journey felt eternal. Papi moved slowly and Julián kept stopping to poke the ground or grab a handful of berries or tap a rhythm against a tree trunk.

"Hurry. Up," Valentina ground out.

Her head thrummed with the erratic beating of her heart. The longer they trekked, the more the pressure built inside her. Finally, she couldn't stand it anymore. Her legs buckled and she stumbled, gasping for air.

"Valentina!" Papi exclaimed, steadying her.

"What's wrong with you?" her brother asked.

Valentina couldn't answer. Her eyes blurred. A single thought broke through the chaos in her head: *We're not going to make it.*

Then the earth began to shake.

THREE

It wasn't a small tremor, like Valentina sometimes felt in the finca. Tremors came with living in the mountains. She hated the sensation—it made her feel all weird and wobbly—but she was used to it.

This was different.

The earth jerked again, harder, sending Valentina and Julián toppling down with a scream. Papi gathered them in his arms. Valentina couldn't breathe. Jolt after jolt shuddered beneath her, leaving her belly flip-flopping. Trees shook like rag dolls. Branches snapped off like twigs. She ducked closer to Papi, covering her head with her arms.

The ground groaned, as if the mountain itself were in pain.

Valentina squeezed her eyes shut. *Please stop. Please stop. Please stop.* They were going to get crushed. Her mind immediately went to the destruction in Medellín last year, when a massive earthquake tore through the city. Buildings crushed. People trapped. Bridges broken. Her mom overwhelmed in the weeks that followed.

Mami! Was she okay? How far was this earthquake being felt? Mami's labs in Manizales were usually structurally sound, but nothing was 100 percent earthquake proof.

Julián burrowed closer to Papi. "Make it stop!"

Valentina instinctively reached for her brother. He didn't pull away.

"It's okay, m'ijo," Papi said. "Stay down. It'll be over soon."

After what felt like centuries, the shaking stopped. They sat in the silence that followed. Valentina pressed her forehead against Papi's chest, letting his scent of sweat and coffee comfort her.

"Everything's fine," Papi murmured. "We're fine. If we're going to go through a big one, I guess this is the way to do it."

A big one. How strong had the earthquake been?

"Mami?" Valentina asked.

Papi pulled away and fished out his cell phone. "No reception. The towers must be down." He tried to give them a reassuring smile. "I'm sure she's fine. She would've seen it coming and gotten to safety. *If* the quake even reached her."

"I want to go home," Julián said. A frown replaced his usual mischievous grin.

"Me too." Valentina wasn't proud that her voice hitched a tiny bit.

Papi nodded. "Vamos, but we have to move carefully. We don't know what the roads are like, if the bridges are still standing, or if there have been landslides. The last thing we need is to get hurt."

They stood up and started walking toward the road again, moving up the mountain slower than before. Papi took a few paces at a time, using a fallen branch to tap the ground before stepping on it. Valentina stayed close behind him, with Julián beside her.

Evidence of the earthquake littered the mountain. Trees lay scattered in their path, their dirt-covered roots reaching toward the sky. In some spots, gaping holes stared back at them, as if a giant had taken a bite out of the Andes. The entire landscape held its breath. No coati whistled. No mountain tapir shrieked. No birds chirped. The only sounds came from Valentina's labored breathing, Julián's grunts, and Papi's soothing murmurs.

"Cuidado," Papi said in one spot, pointing to a large tree sprawled ahead of them. They climbed carefully over it and kept hiking.

The closer they got to their parked truck, the more the pressure in Valentina's chest eased. Soon, she was taking in huge gulps of air. Relief mingled with confusion. Had she had a premonition? That made about as much sense as searching for a patasola, but she couldn't deny the sensations before the earthquake. She'd file that away for later, when she was home, curled up safely in bed.

"Why's the madremonte so mad at us?" Julián asked after the fifth fallen tree they passed.

Papi chuckled under his breath, tapping with his branch as he walked. "I suppose we won't know unless we find her and ask."

Valentina was too tired to argue. Leave it to her brother to bring up another mythical creature at a time like this. "Maybe she's tired of people being jerks," she said dryly.

According to legends, the madremonte protected jungles, rivers, and mountains. She was the mother of the land, tall and imposing, with moss for hair, a crown of leaves, and bright glowing eyes. She commanded the earth, wind, and rain—but when people harmed the land? ¡Cuidado! She unleashed her rage. Mudslides, floods, and earthquakes were all blamed on the madremonte. Papi always said she was his favorite because she kept the world in balance.

"Wait." Papi stopped suddenly, spreading out his arms to keep them back. "The ground is unsteady. Miren."

Valentina looked where Papi pointed. Several cracks zigzagged across the dry earth, shifting as if the earth were breathing. A few paces to their left, the cracks widened enough to fit a man. The uneasiness returned as Valentina remembered her nightmare.

"Let me see." Julián pushed in front of her. "Was that from the earthquake?"

Papi nodded. "We're lucky there wasn't un derrumbe."

Valentina shuddered, not wanting to think what would've happened if they'd been caught in a landslide.

"We're close to the truck." Papi poked at the dirt with the branch. It fell away easily, like sand. Valentina was about to suggest jumping over the crack when her skin tingled, her stomach recoiled, and she broke out into a cold sweat.

"It's going to happen again," she whispered.

"What?" Julián said. Papi whipped around and stared at her.

"Another earthquake—"

The earth gave a sharp jolt and the crevice before them widened, splitting outward like branches off a river. The cracks groaned as the ground fell away.

Just like in her dream.

No!

She stood frozen, her feet growing into roots. She barely heard Julián's cries. She could only stare into the darkness before her.

"Get back!" Papi yanked her arm.

She scrambled away, pulling her brother with her. But now, Papi stood too close to the yawning mouth that kept growing, trying to devour them. She screamed as Papi stumbled, his walking stick tumbling from his hands. Then he was falling, eyes wide with the terror she felt, his lips forming words she didn't hear.

A deep rumbling echoed around them. Then the mountain hushed once more.

FOUR

"Papi!" Julián cried.

Silence.

Valentina stared at the spot where their dad had disappeared, waiting for him to pop up and say, "Gotcha!"

This was a dream. It had to be.

But no: the sway of the earth beneath her, the horror of watching Papi tumble, the desperation clawing its way up her throat—those were all real.

Julián darted toward the crevice, but Valentina yanked him back before he got too close.

"*Think*, Julián," she snapped. "If we're not careful, we fall too."

He glared at her. "We can't do nothing."

She studied the cracked earth and the trees around them. *Think*, she told herself. If they stood too close, they'd fall. If they didn't, they wouldn't know if Papi was okay. *Think, think, think*. Then she remembered the emergency supplies in her mochila. Quickly, she dumped the contents on the ground. She had a flashlight, a first aid kit, an extra canteen with water, and rope. She could kiss her father right now—she would never ever complain about packing these again!

"We'll use the rope," she said, a plan forming in her head. She tied one end tight around the trunk of a nearby tree, like Papi had shown her. Then she tied the other end around her waist. "You stay here."

"Let me do it," her brother said.

Valentina shook her head. "I'm bigger and can pull him up easier. If something happens to me . . ." She took a deep breath. "Then you can go get help. No use both of us getting stuck down there with him. If Papi's okay, if he's not too far down, we can pull him up."

Her brother scowled. "Fine."

Valentina dropped on her belly and began crawling forward. She hoped this would be enough, that the ground would hold steady. She'd be okay if her knots didn't fall apart, but what about Papi? What if he was unconscious—or worse?

She shoved those thoughts away and concentrated on the task. She crept toward the edge of the crevice, and she swore she heard the earth beneath her shift and sigh. The musky scent of dirt and leaves made her stomach churn.

"Faster," Julián called.

Valentina grunted. "Shut up and let me concentrate."

Almost there. After what felt like eons, she poked her head over the edge. And sucked in a breath. Papi lay sprawled on a rocky ledge.

"Papi!" she screamed, then to her brother, "I see him!" She scanned the drop. He was too far down to reach, even with the rope.

"Is he okay?" Julián asked.

Papi groaned, shifting to his side.

"He's alive!" she said.

"So what are you waiting for?" She heard the impatience in his voice. Why did he always have to rush into things?

"I can't reach him."

A wave of hopelessness washed over her. There was no one around to help, and they couldn't reach him on their own. They had to leave him. It was the only way, but the thought left her breathless.

"Papi, can you hear me? We're going to find help." Then, more softly, "Te amo." He didn't respond.

Valentina scooted back, quicker now that she felt confident the earth wouldn't crumble around her. When she reached her brother, the first words out of his mouth were: "We have to save him."

"I know."

Valentina had never hiked through the mountains on her own. All she knew came from Papi's stories and lessons. He'd always drilled them on how easy it was to get lost in the jungle. You could guide yourself with the sun and a compass, but without either, the trees all began to look the same after a while. How were they supposed to leave Papi, hike the rest of the way up to the road, get help, and then make their way back to him? What if they took a wrong turn? What if they couldn't find him again?

Valentina felt the panic spreading to her fingertips. Her breaths came quick and hard. *Stop it!* she told herself. She had to stay focused. She and Julián had to get this right.

Their father's life depended on it.

"Vale?" Julián's eyebrows furrowed. His face was streaked with sweat and dirt.

"Up," Valentina said finally. "We find the car, we find help." They'd parked by a small, rustic restaurant with a burned-out Coca-Cola sign and peeling yellow paint. The owners of the restaurant would help. They had to.

Her brother pulled her up. While Julián packed the scattered items into the mochila, Valentina picked at the knotted rope around her waist. After a few tries, it fell limp to the ground and she moved on to the knot around the tree.

"We need something to mark our way back," Valentina said as Julián handed her the mochila.

He glanced around. "How about this?" He picked up a rock and started rubbing the bark of the tree until a dark circle was etched on the trunk.

Valentina nodded. "That works." She hoped it was enough.

Then she sent a silent kiss toward Papi, and they moved away from the crevice, searching for solid ground so they could continue their climb upward, toward the road.

They'd only taken a few steps, though, when the ground collapsed beneath them. Valentina screamed as they fell through dirt and leaves and rocks.

An eternity later, she crashed hard against the bottom with an "Oof!"

She lay on her back, trying to breathe. Everything hurt. Pain meant she was still alive, right? She took in a deep breath, only to dissolve into a coughing fit from the cloud of dirt surrounding her.

A groan sounded nearby.

"Julián!" Valentina covered her nose and mouth with the top of her T-shirt and crawled over to him. Her hands stung. "Julián," she said again when she reached him. He looked as dusty as she felt.

"Are we alive?" He winced as he sat up.

"Yeah." Valentina glanced toward the spot where they'd just been standing. How far down had they fallen? At least one story. It was a miracle they weren't seriously hurt.

Julián followed her gaze. "How're we getting out of here?"

Valentina didn't miss the small tremor in his voice. "I don't know yet."

She stood up and took in their surroundings. They were in a pit of some sort, but this looked different from where Papi had fallen. That had been all emptiness except for the ledge. This space, however, felt more like a hollow within the mountain, with dirt walls that looked carved by humans, not made by an earthquake. They were covered with markings.

"Mira," Valentina said, pointing.

Julián came to stand beside her. "What's that?"

"I think they're drawings."

She couldn't be sure, though. She picked up her mochila, which lay a few paces away, and rummaged through it until she found the flashlight.

Valentina swept the light over the space. A collection of stone slabs sat ahead, reminding her of weather-worn and forgotten ruins, like those of la Ciudad Perdida, near Santa Marta.

"Whoa," Julián breathed. "Where *are* we?"

Valentina shook her head. She had no idea.

Above her, she could make out two columns of hard-packed dirt reaching toward each other. Two ends of an arch, she realized. The top must've gotten dislodged in the earthquake. Her gaze settled on a mound of soil in front of her. Yep—an arch separating this space from the mountain above.

And they were the unlucky ones to fall through it.

What if another tremor rattled this section and the walls caved in on them? They had rope, but without trees or rocks or anything to hook the rope onto, it was useless. If they stayed stuck down here, they would run out of food and water, and so would Papi. The more she studied her surroundings, the more fear bunched into a knot at her throat. Who was going to help them if no one knew where they were?

Stay calm. That's what Papi would say.

"Look for something to grab on to. Maybe some stones or roots or—" Valentina broke off as her light fell on a boulder tucked into the smooth dirt behind her. She moved closer. All around the rock were upside-down *V*s with circles above them and numbers inside the circles. She placed her finger on the grooves.

"That's so cool," her brother said. "It's like the entrance to an underground lair."

"We don't have time for cool," Valentina said. "We need a way out."

"Maybe this is it," Julián said, hands on hips, looking the way Mami often did when she was exasperated with them. "Maybe there's a cave behind it that could be our way out."

"Caves don't have exits. They're dead ends."

"Some do. I saw it on one of those nature documentaries Mami likes to watch."

Valentina looked at him doubtfully.

"Do you have a better idea?"

She didn't. So much could go wrong. If this *was* a way out, who knew where it would lead them. They could get lost, coming out in an unknown part of the jungle. She swept the flashlight again through the space, only to come back to the boulder with the weird markings. She sighed. Julián was right. Staying here was not an option.

"Fine," she said. "Help me move this boulder."

Julián stood beside her and together, they placed their hands on it.

"On the count of three," Valentina said. "Uno . . . dos . . ."

She didn't get to "tres" because, just then, the boulder rolled aside with a rumble, revealing the dark, yawning mouth of the cave.

FIVE

Valentina and Julián stared at each other.

"What just happened?" Valentina asked.

"Magic?" Though Julián's face was pale, his eyes glittered. He took a step toward the cave, but Valentina grabbed his shirt.

"You can't just run in there!"

She stared at the opening. This could be a terrible, horrible mistake. There could be snakes, scorpions, or other poisonous animals in there. But what choice did they have? Papi was hurt, and they couldn't find help while stuck in this stupid pit.

"We go in *slowly*," Valentina said. "We don't know what's in there or if the earthquake rattled anything."

"Whatever you say, O great one," Julián said, and though he sighed when she took his hand, he didn't pull away. He seemed ready to investigate the cave no matter the cost.

Please let this be our way out, Valentina thought as they crossed the threshold together.

Inside, steaming heat rose from the ground. With the light of the flashlight, Valentina saw roots wiggling down the walls, pale veins against black dirt. In the distance, a drip, drip, drip echoed everywhere and nowhere all at once.

The cave reminded her more of an underground tunnel than some animal's home. For the first time since the earthquake, she felt hope. A tunnel could definitely lead them out toward help.

"Whoa," Julián said.

"I know."

Without warning, the ground rumbled. At first, Valentina thought it was another aftershock, but as she watched in horror, the boulder rolled back into its resting spot, shutting them in.

"No!" Valentina yelled, dropping her flashlight. It fell with a plunk, shuddering off and snuffing out the light. Complete darkness covered them. She pushed the rock with all her strength.

It didn't budge.

"No, no, no," she groaned.

A beam of light clicked on, bouncing slightly against the cavernous walls. Julián's hands shook as he gripped the flashlight.

"Help me!" Valentina cried, continuing to push. Nothing happened. The boulder remained jammed in the mouth of the cave.

"Stop it!" Julián's voice trembled a little. "We can't even get out that way, remember?"

Valentina slid down on the hard earth. How could her brother be so reasonable? She tried to beat the panic rising in her chest. He was right. They had planned to find a way out through the cave. The boulder sealing them in didn't change that.

Except if there isn't an exit, we'll be buried in the mountain alive.

Julián crouched in front of her. "C'mon, Vale."

She closed her eyes and inhaled. A subtle scent of salt saturated the space, reminding her of the salt mine they'd visited in Zipaquirá on their last family vacation. Papi had been so excited, narrating the history of the underground church carved from the salt.

Papi . . . Valentina stood, wiping her hands on her jeans. Her palms were slick with sweat and blood from scrapes.

"Let's go," she said.

Julián nodded and handed her the flashlight. She could see the fear in his eyes. He wouldn't admit how scared he was, not to her, but she knew her brother. She had to keep calm for him.

They moved slowly, each step measured and unsure. While the flashlight illuminated the space in front of them for a few feet, the rest of the cave resembled a black hole. The deeper they went, the louder the drip-drip-drip got. The jagged roof above them jutted down, at times so much they had to duck to get through. In other spots, it was higher than their house. The pale roots, which were sparse at first, multiplied now. They reminded Valentina of snakes. She half expected them to jump off the walls and slither toward her.

After a while, Julián stopped and pointed. "Do you see that?"

She didn't see anything except complete darkness. "What?"

"Keep looking."

She narrowed her eyes. "There's nothing—"

Only there *was* something. Sparks of light lit up what had only been total darkness before. Not a whole lot, more like the subtle hint of sunrise. Her heart raced—if there was light, then there might be an exit.

And if there was an exit, they could find help!

She wiped the sweat from her face with her T-shirt. They moved faster now, and Valentina felt lighter than she had since this whole ordeal started. They would get out of this nightmare and find help for Papi.

Soon the tunnel narrowed. A wisp of cool air nipped at her, refreshing after all that heat. Valentina focused on the light ahead of them, which grew brighter the closer they got. When it was light enough to see without the help of the flashlight, she clicked it off and slipped it into her mochila.

She could see the details of the cave walls better now. Packed dirt blended with grainy yellow rock that reminded her of the sands of the Guajira. But the northernmost desert region of Colombia and this part of the Andes were over eight hundred miles apart. Strange. It was as if someone had pulled the thread between both places and smooshed them together.

"C'mon," Julián said, taking off toward the halo of light ahead. "Papi's counting on us."

"Wait!" Valentina tried to keep up with him.

The tunnel ended in a cavern, wider and taller than where they'd started, and she froze, momentarily forgetting everything—even her brother.

Sunlight and water cascaded through a skylight in the roof of the cavern, plunging the space into a kaleidoscope of colors. A small pond lay at the bottom of the waterfall, light and shadows dancing off its surface. Stone sculptures made of the same type of rock as the walls circled the pond. She itched to take out her sketch pad and pencils, to draw this grotto. This was perfect for her portfolio. It was sure to wow Señora Ramirez and earn her a one-way ticket to the Bogotá Academy of Arts.

Maybe after they found help for Papi, she could come back and draw it.

She wandered toward the sculptures, which Valentina now realized resembled different creatures, some otherworldly, others humanlike. Up close, she could see the care with which the artist had carved their faces and bodies. They *looked* real, even the weirdest ones. She recognized some of them from Papi's stories. Her gaze settled on one of a woman with flowing hair trailing behind her. On her head rested a crown of leaves. Valentina would recognize her anywhere—Madremonte.

Was this some kind of shrine to the legends? She wished Papi could see it now.

Valentina stepped closer to the pond and caught her refracted reflection on its surface. The cluster of freckles on her right cheek seemed to shine brighter.

"Mira," Julián said, making her look up. He had moved to an archway a few feet away, and beyond that opening, Valentina saw white light shining on green grass.

They had found a way out!

SIX

Valentina ran to her brother's side and blinked as her eyes adjusted to the unexpected brightness. Sprawling fields of tall grass stretched as far as she could see, pocketed with colorful bursts of magenta, violet, and tangerine. If she squinted enough, she could make out the bushy treetops of a forest in the distance.

How long had they been stumbling through the cave? Thirty minutes? An hour? It should have been late afternoon, but the sun was directly above them, shining down with midday heat. And where was the jungle they'd just been in?

"What—?" she started, but Julián cut her off.

"We found help!"

Valentina turned and saw what had drawn his attention. A small cottage sat to their left. It reminded her of Papi's study on the finca: White stucco walls. Stilts holding it up like a precious jewel. A wrap-around porch, with bright red beams and matching red steps leading toward the grass below. The similarity to home made her heart ache.

On the front porch, pruning some orchids, stood a squat little woman with a long, flowy dress and a neat, pointed hat. Wisps of gray-streaked black hair tumbled down her back.

Valentina hesitated. "I don't know."

"Don't you want to save Papi?" Julián said.

"Of course I do," she said. "But something weird's going on."

"Whatever." Before Valentina could do anything, Julián jogged away, calling out, "¡Hola! We need your help!"

Valentina scowled but followed him anyway.

As Julián approached, the woman paused her pruning and tilted her head. She didn't say anything, but her bright eyes watched them curiously.

"We need help," her brother repeated. "Our dad got hurt in the earthquake. . . ."

As Julián spoke, Valentina hung back, studying their surroundings. That was when she realized there was no sign of the earthquake or the drought they'd left behind. She turned in a circle, her confusion giving way to alarm. The cave they'd just exited was *not* carved into the side of a mountain, as it had been in the jungle. Instead, a small mound of earth surrounded the opening, blending into a sea of golden sand dunes behind it.

The Andes Mountains had completely disappeared.

Impossible. Maybe she'd hit her head harder than she thought.

"Oh dear," the woman was saying, her voice tinkling like wind chimes. The topmost point of her hat twitched. "I thought I felt the pop of the border, but I thought to myself, 'Grucinda, you old bat. There's no way someone could've gotten past the enchantments. It's preposterous!'" She slipped the shears into a basket and wiped her hands on her apron.

"Um, I'm sorry. What?" Valentina exchanged a glance with her brother, who shrugged. When she looked back at the odd woman, she was standing right in front of them on the grass. Valentina yelped, taking a reflexive step backward. Up close, the woman—Grucinda?—was only a couple inches taller than Valentina.

"And yet here you are," Grucinda continued. "First humans to grace our land since that awful, awful time. It's been hundreds of years. Does our queen know?"

Julián stared at the woman intently, his brows furrowed. It was the same expression he wore when he played chess with their abuelito.

"Where did I go wrong?" Grucinda said. She paced before them, shaking her head as she spoke. "If they find out, it's going to be the death of me."

"Please," Valentina said, cutting her off. "We need your help to get to our father."

"Oh dear, oh dear. I'm afraid it's not possible," Grucinda said, stopping before them. Her expression softened. "Once you passed through the border, it sealed shut. There's no way back to your world."

"What?" Valentina and Julián said at the same time.

"This isn't funny." Valentina's voice hitched. That was all they needed—to end up at the mercy of a crazy old woman when she was the only one able to help them. They'd never get to Papi this way. Valentina scanned the area, looking for another house to find help, but there was none. This cottage was the only sign of life on this flat landscape.

She whirled around to face her brother. "This is your fault. If you hadn't moved around so much, maybe the ground would've held."

"My fault?" Julián's face turned bright red. "You're the one who did something freaky and brought the earthquake."

Valentina recoiled. "I. Did. *Not*. Have anything to do with the earthquake."

Grucinda had been studying them, her fingers tapping the flap of her hat. Now she screeched, "Silence!" and with a flick of her wrists, she froze Valentina and Julián in place.

Valentina's heart thudded in terror as she struggled to move. Suddenly, thick, plasticlike sheets crisscrossed around them, encasing them in a bubble a few feet off the ground. She opened her mouth to shout, but no sound came out. Julián stared wide-eyed, his mouth also forming soundless words. When the last sheet clicked into place, whatever force was holding them frozen relaxed, and Valentina tumbled to her knees as she hit the bottom of the bubble. It was surprisingly soft, but that did nothing to calm her.

"What the heck?" she screamed, her voice coming back. "Let us out!"

But Julián looked strangely triumphant beside her. "I knew it!" He pointed at Grucinda. "You're the brujita from Papi's stories!"

Valentina groaned. "Don't start with this." They needed to get free.

Grucinda's eyes narrowed.

"Look at her," Julián insisted. "Her hat, her house—everything is just like he said! Vale, she just did *magic*!"

Papi's studio cottage was called "La casita de la bruja" back home. Papi claimed the brujita loved nature and her people, used her gifts to heal and help, and always had bowls of candy for kids even though she didn't have any kids of her own. Most other people Valentina knew told a different story: brujas were witches who had sold their souls to the devil and spent their nights stealing kids and leading people away from good.

Valentina didn't believe in either version.

But as Grucinda harrumphed, turning on her heel and pulling them along in their floating bubble—up the steps, onto the porch, and into her cottage—Valentina couldn't deny the impossible was happening.

The last glimpse she had was of the cave's entrance dissolving into the golden earth as the cottage door shut and the lock clicked.

SEVEN

"I have quite a few questions for you two," Grucinda said once they were inside.

"*You* have questions?!" Valentina said.

"You can't keep us in here!" Julián bounced against the walls of the bubble, as if that alone could shatter this prison.

Grucinda ignored them. "How did you break through my enchantments and into Tierra de los Olvidados?"

Land of the Forgotten? What a strange name for this place. Valentina had never heard of such a thing, not even in Papi's stories.

"And how on this tierrita did you know I was a bruja?" Grucinda continued.

Julián paused in his attempts to break the bubble. "See? She's real!"

There's no such thing. But between the disappearing Andes and this floating prison, Valentina couldn't muster another protest. The world was upside down. Papi was in danger, and they were nowhere near to getting him help. Instead, they were trapped in a strange place with a strange woman. A bruja. Sure, why not?

Grucinda approached them and inhaled deeply. "Interesante."

Was she smelling them? Gross. Valentina leaned as far back as she could, but it was pointless. She had nowhere to go.

"That's just wrong," Julián said. "I could've farted."

Valentina buried her head in her hands. *Think*, she ordered herself. They needed to escape. But how? The cave opening had just *disappeared*, and the brujita had bubble-wrapped them.

Valentina glanced at Grucinda. "Please let us out," she pleaded. "I don't know where we are or how we got here exactly. When the earthquake hit, we fell and found a tunnel. We thought it was a way out. If we don't help our dad soon, he might die!" Her voice trembled because, despite them needing to convince Grucinda, it was the truth. If they didn't get out, Papi was as good as gone. And she couldn't deal with *that* truth. Not now. Not ever.

The woman's features softened slightly. "I'm sorry. What I said still stands. This border has sealed shut. I do not have the power to reopen it."

"So we can't go home?" Julián's excitement disappeared.

"Now, I didn't say that." Grucinda's gaze skittered around as she paced, her lips pressed in a straight line.

Valentina followed the little witch with her eyes, and as she did, she noticed the space around them for the first time.

They were in a colorful living room with a mustard-yellow wicker sofa, deep-coral cushions, and bright red-orange walls covered with paintings of rainbow rivers, snowcapped mountains, and shimmering hummingbirds that *actually* moved! In a corner, a large face-shaped clock hung suspended in the air, eyes closed and a soft snore slipping from its number six. A broom hovered above the floor in the middle of the room, and the flowers by the window shook themselves like wet dogs as water sprinkled over them from the ceiling.

Despite their predicament, her fingers itched to draw it all.

A splendid scent of cinnamon and roses and peppermint invaded their bubble, reminding her of Doña Alicia's cooking and Abuelita's home remedies, of Mami and Papi.

They needed to get out.

"Please," Valentina whispered. "Help us help our father. How do we get back home?"

Grucinda sighed. "There's only one working portal on this land, and it's in our queen's castle. Madremonte guards it closely because she believes it's where her son will return." The little witch's hands flew to her mouth. "Oh dear, I've said too much."

Julián perked up. "The madremonte's real too?"

And she has a son? This was the first Valentina had heard of such a thing. According to Papi and to "official" accounts, the madremonte was a lonely creature who protected the earth and who hunted down those who hurt it. While she might be known as Mother Mountain, she wasn't known as a *literal* mom.

The brujita's eyes narrowed again. "How do you know so much about our kind?"

Julián shrugged. "Lots of people believe in you and the other legends."

That's stretching the truth a bit, Valentina thought.

Grucinda straightened in surprise, so fast her hat fell askew. "They still believe in us? After all these years?"

"Well, some of us do," Julián amended, shooting Valentina a pointed look.

Valentina scowled and pressed her mochila against her chest. She'd had enough. If the only way home was through the madremonte, then that was where they needed to go. But first they needed to get out of the brujita's bubble.

The hard angle of Papi's emergency tool kit in her bag gave her an idea. "I'm hungry," she said. "Do you have anything to eat?"

"And something to drink, please!" Julián piped up. "I ran out of water in the tunnel."

Grucinda paused. "I suppose I can whip up something. Wasn't

expecting company, you see." She tapped her hat pensively. "Now, what do a pair of human children eat and drink?"

Valentina bristled at being called a child.

"Um, nothing that's alive?" Julián said.

This made Grucinda laugh. "Oh dear. We don't eat anything alive either. Hold tight. I'll be right back."

And with that, she disappeared through an archway on the far end of the living room, humming a lively melody.

The moment Grucinda was out of view, Valentina dropped to her knees and slipped off her mochila. "We need to get out," she told Julián as she rummaged through her stuff until she found what she was looking for. Papi's utility knife.

"Duh." He dropped beside her.

Before they could begin trying to cut their way out of the plexiglass-like bubble, though, the wall clock snorted awake and chimed in a loud, squeaking voice: "Madremonte's guard Patasola has left the castle and is on her way."

EIGHT

"The patasola!" Julián hissed.

Yeah, Valentina had heard. She felt a pang as she remembered Papi tracking the patasola in the Andes. It was the reason they were in this mess in the first place. And here they were, about to actually meet her.

Grucinda came rushing in, her eyes wild, hat askew. "She can't know you're here! If she knows you've crossed over and I didn't report you right away—oh!" She had just seen them crouched on the bottom of the bubble, incriminating utility knife in hand.

Valentina opened her mouth, but before she could make up an excuse, Grucinda snapped her fingers. In an instant, the bubble disappeared, and Valentina and Julián tumbled to the ground.

"*Ouch.* Thanks a lot," Julián grumbled.

"We don't have time. You need to leave," Grucinda said.

Valentina crossed her arms. "That's what we've been saying."

Grucinda darted back toward the kitchen, calling over her shoulder, "Follow me."

Julián bounded after the witch, but Valentina hesitated. If the patasola was Madremonte's guard, shouldn't they stay? After all, if the queen was the key to getting to Papi, then it would save them the trouble of having to find her.

The witch poked her head out from the archway. "If you wish to live and save your father, you need to come here *now*."

That made Valentina move.

In the small kitchen, the brujita rushed around like a dog chasing its tail.

"There's not much time," Grucinda said, grabbing two cloth bags. She snapped her fingers, filling each with bread, cheese, fruits, and nuts. Another snap of her fingers had Valentina's and Julián's waterskins flying from their mochilas. Water filled them an instant later. With a third snap, everything returned to its place without Valentina and Julián having to move a finger.

"What's the big deal?" Julián asked.

"Heed my every word," Grucinda said, leaning in close. "The portal is in Madremonte's castle, but she guards it carefully. You will need to seek her and convince her to help you. The only way you can go home and save your father is through our queen."

Valentina frowned. "Then why are you sending us away? Just hand us over to her guard."

Grucinda's expression darkened. "There is an explicit order to capture and eliminate any humans who come onto our land." She laughed humorlessly. "Foolishness. But here we are. I sealed my fate the moment I did not report you. If Her Majesty's guard finds you, you will die, and I shall be imprisoned."

Julián made a strangled noise.

"If the madremonte wants us dead," Valentina asked, "how are we supposed to convince her before she kills us?" This was beginning to sound like an impossible mission.

"I know our queen," Grucinda said hastily. "She may be heartbroken, but she was never heartless, no matter what she's done since then. The element of surprise, I believe, will offer you the space to persuade her."

The wall clock whined, "Madremonte's guard Patasola will be here in sixty heartbeats."

"Oh dear, oh dear!" Grucinda snapped her fingers, and a piece of parchment appeared, which the brujita handed to Valentina. A map.

"Let me see," Julián complained.

Valentina shifted to make room for her brother.

"This is my home." Grucinda pointed at the image of a small cottage on the bottom left-hand corner, which sat between two rivers and which was surrounded by desert on one side, grassy fields on the other. "Take the Río de Mil Colores to the Bosque de Sueños, and travel through the forest until you reach the Cordillera Monumental. Our queen lives there in the mountains." She tapped the picture of a castle in the upper right-hand corner of the map, where a small compass marked north.

It wasn't lost on Valentina that this map seemed like a mirror image of Colombia. But she didn't have time to dwell on it. She nodded and said, "River of a Thousand Colors, Forest of Dreams, Monumental Mountain Range. Got it." Inside, though, she groaned at the thought of trekking through more jungles and mountains.

"Madremonte's guard will be here in forty heartbeats," the wall clock squeaked.

Grucinda yanked open a door that had materialized beside one of the large cabinets. "Come, children."

Valentina saw rows and rows of guadua, tall bamboo stalks with leafy clusters at the top. Shadows danced between them.

"I don't know," Valentina said, gripping her mochila tight. Her heart thudded. She'd grown used to this little witch, despite everything. She didn't exactly want to go looking for a heartbroken, murderous queen who might kill them the instant she saw them. But if that was the only way to save Papi, they had to try. And if Grucinda was telling the truth, it would be even more dangerous to stick around and wait for the patasola.

"Madremonte's guard will be here in twenty heartbeats!" the wall clock moaned.

"Go through this bamboo forest," Grucinda said. "Find the Dragon of the River. He can be trusted to help you. And when you see Madremonte, remind her of the love she felt once for *all* living creatures—regardless of species. She won't listen to me, but perhaps she'll listen to you."

Now the wall clock screeched: "Madremonte's guard will be here in two heartbeats!"

"Go!" Grucinda said, pushing them out the door. "Save yourselves and your father!"

NINE

The door slammed shut just as a loud suction noise and *pop* sounded from the front of the cottage. Almost instantly, the door in front of them disappeared, replaced instead by a solid wall made of slats of white wood. There was no way back inside from where they stood.

"Did that just happen?" Valentina asked.

"I think so?" Julián said.

Muffled voices floated through the wall. Julián pressed his ear against the wood, and Valentina instinctively reached out to pull him back but paused. Why shouldn't they eavesdrop? It might give them clues that could help them convince Madremonte when they met her.

Valentina joined her brother, closing her eyes to focus on the voices. She could just make out Grucinda saying, "To what do I owe this unexpected visit?"

The voice that answered sent shivers down to Valentina's toes. It was low and cold, the kind of sound you didn't want to hear when you were alone and in the dark. "Don't toy with me, Grucinda. You knew perfectly well I was coming, thanks to that cursed clock of yours."

"Nonsense."

A shuffle, and then the patasola's voice came much closer. "The alarm on the border went off."

Valentina cringed, fighting the urge to step back. *She can't see us.*

"Did it, now?" Grucinda said. "And what does that have to do with me?"

The patasola all but growled, "It came from the portal near your house."

"How is that even possible? This border was sealed shut after the young prince's disappearance—on your orders. It's been ages. Are you certain it was not a false alarm?"

The guard's voice came dangerously low. "You know as well as anyone that the magic protecting our borders does not lend itself to *false* alarms."

"Then this news is quite peculiar, indeed."

Valentina couldn't help agreeing. It *was* all incredibly odd. How did a portal that was sealed by a brujita's magic let them into Tierra de los Olvidados?

"Have you noticed anything strange around here?" the guard asked.

"Nothing save for a pack of rotten mice who keep stealing my stash of candy."

Valentina bit back a giggle at Grucinda's audacity. She didn't want to imagine the patasola's expression, though she certainly heard the disdain in her voice when the guard ground out, "This is not a joke, Grucinda."

Their voices grew fainter, and Valentina couldn't hear them through the wall. She pressed in, hoping to hear more, when suddenly the patasola's shrill voice rang out, "Then you won't mind my searching your property!"

Valentina pushed off as if burned. "We need to go." She glanced at her brother, who was still pressed to the wall, eyes shut in concentration. "Seriously." Valentina tugged on his shirt. Julián batted her hand away. "We need to go."

Just then, Grucinda's voice came through loud and clear.

"Unhand me! How dare you come into my house and arrest me! Just because you're Madremonte's right hand does *not* give you the right to—AY!"

Terror tore through Valentina. Should they go in and help Grucinda? But how? They could barely help themselves. Besides, if Grucinda was right, they were as good as dead if the patasola caught them.

Valentina began backing away from the cottage, dragging her brother with her. This time, he didn't struggle. His face had paled. In the next instant, the front door of the cottage slammed closed.

"Run!" she breathed.

Julián didn't need to be told twice. They darted into the bamboo forest, and Valentina barely paid attention to the creatures scurrying away from them, scattering into their holes.

Find the Dragon of the River.

That was what Grucinda had said. Through the forest to the waterway. There they would find the dragon. Her mochila banged against her as she ran, but she didn't stop. Neither did her brother.

They ran as if their lives depended on it—because they did.

TEN

Valentina and Julián ran until the tall stalks of bamboo thinned and they caught the glimmer of sunlight on water in the distance, like a wonderful mirage.

"We're . . . almost . . . there. . . ." She slowed to a walk.

"Don't stop," Julián said, tugging her arm.

Valentina shook her head. "I don't think she followed us." The only sounds came from the shifting of leaves in the warm breeze and the whistling of birds in the treetops. When she looked back, she couldn't even glimpse the brujita's house through the guadua.

Julián slowed now. "Are you sure?"

"Positive." It was more like "pretty sure," but she wouldn't tell her brother that.

They walked in silence for a few beats before he asked, "Should we have helped her?"

"How?" Try as she might, Valentina couldn't keep the despair from her voice. "We don't have weapons, and if a magical witch couldn't stand up to the patasola, how could we?"

More silence stretched between them as the reality of what they'd left behind weighed on their shoulders.

"Will Grucinda be okay?" Julián asked.

Valentina turned and met his worried gaze. With the light streaming in through the trees, her brother seemed to be glowing. "Look, the patasola wouldn't have killed Grucinda—only us. She'll put Grucinda in jail, but we'll get her out. We'll go to

Madremonte and convince her, okay? We'll make sure of it."

Her brother pressed his lips together and nodded.

"Good. Now let's find this 'Dragon of the River.'"

They walked through the last brittle trunks and onto soft grass, and Valentina stopped short. Pink clouds dotted the sky. Gone were the shadows of bamboo. Instead, an expanse of grass-lands with pockets of deep greens and golds stretched before her, interrupted only by a few solitary trees and a wide, snaking river with sunlight sparkling off it. The landscape reminded Valentina so much of the Llanos Orientales, the plains and wetlands that stretched east from the foot of the Andes toward Venezuela.

Tierra de los Olvidados seemed to be the ghost of Colombia—a thought that sent a pang through her. She missed her home, her mountains, her family. She missed Papi's obsession with magical creatures, which didn't seem so silly now. Why had she doubted him? She would give anything to see him again, to tell him he'd been right and that she would never ever question him again.

"Do you think the dragon is the one from Papi's stories?" Julián asked. "The lake monster?"

Valentina laughed. "Maybe." The brujita seemed to be just like the one from his stories, so it was quite possible the dragon was too.

The lake monster was a creature from Lake Tota, in the mountains northeast of Bogotá. Legends said a creature lurked beneath the waters. It was sometimes called "diablo ballena," or "devil whale," and it terrified everyone. Papi's stories about this monster, like those of the brujita, differed from local legends. His monster was kind and playful, *not* bent on taking people into a watery grave.

So if Grucinda was good and she said to trust the Dragon of the River, then Valentina would trust him. Hopefully he wouldn't be as terrifying as legends described him, a dragon the size of a whale with the head of an ox and blazing eyes that would devour you in a single bite.

Valentina did *not* want to think about that.

The soft grass thinned into a gray sandy beach beside the ambling river, which burst into an explosion of fuchsia, indigo, teal, and tangerine. The brilliant colors swirled within the water like a liquid rainbow and coated the terra-cotta rocks peeking out. In Colombia, a similar rainbow river existed. Valentina had never seen Caño Cristales in person, but Mami had told her about the algae and other plants that bloomed yearly and that gave the river its colors.

Here in this land, was it science or magic that gave the Río de Mil Colores its brilliant hues?

Valentina studied the river. It was too wide to cross but slow moving. Still, if Papi had taught her anything, it was that you could never let your guard down around a body of water.

"Keep your eyes open," Valentina said, keeping a safe distance. "The dragon should be in the river."

"Wow," her brother said. "Big brains."

"Shut up," Valentina snapped. "You don't have to be such a brat about it." She was tired, her legs felt like spaghetti from all the running, and she missed home with a fierce ache. She sucked in a breath and counted to ten, trying to get her frustration under control.

"Sorry," Julián mumbled. He squinted toward the water. "Why don't we just call the dragon?"

Valentina opened her mouth to say that was a dumb idea but then closed it, because she couldn't think of anything else, and he was trying to help. "Okay," she said slowly. "How do we call him?"

"Just watch the master." He darted toward the edge before she could stop him.

"Julián!" She ran after him. "¡Para!"

But her brother ignored her and instead dropped to his knees. He leaned in and spoke words she couldn't hear. Suddenly, the water began churning and bubbling, white foam building in the center of the river.

She yanked him up. "What did you do?"

He shrugged. "I just asked if the dragon could come help us because Grucinda was in trouble and so were we."

"And it worked?" Valentina asked.

"Duh." He pointed to the river with a satisfied smirk.

They stood side by side, watching as the foam cleared around a gray head, elongated snout, and pointed ears. Then, a long and slender neck rose out of the water, followed by a wide body with sharp fins down the back and a pair of scaly, iridescent wings on either side. Finally, a snakelike tail slithered across the river's surface.

Valentina gasped, rooted to the wet dirt as the dragon slowly turned his head toward them.

ELEVEN

Valentina stared into the beady black eyes of the infamous diablo ballena and gulped. She couldn't move. Even her mind went blank. From the corner of her eye, she saw her brother inching closer to the dragon. That spurred her into action.

"Julián!" Valentina shrieked. "What're you doing?"

"I'm walking on water. What does it look like I'm doing?"

"STOP!"

He rolled his eyes. "The brujita said we could trust him." He crossed the last few steps until he was beside the towering beast.

"I'm going to kill you," Valentina muttered. Sure, Grucinda had said that, and they sort of trusted *her*. But what if Grucinda was wrong? What if this dragon felt the same way about them as the patasola and madremonte did? This could be a terrible, horrible mistake and the beast would tear them limb from limb, devouring them.

No matter how bratty Julián might be, he was still her brother, and she had to keep him safe. Before she could change her mind, she darted in front of her brother and threw her arms out. "Please don't eat us!"

The diablo ballena's jaw opened wide, and an unearthly deep voice boomed: "WHO DARES DISTURB THE DRAGON OF THE RIVER?"

Valentina felt every hair on her body stand up. Even her brother paled and took a reflexive step backward. But then the monster did the strangest thing. He tossed his head and . . . laughed? The devil whale roared with laughter, slapping his tail on the water's surface, sending a kaleidoscope of color in every direction.

"Oh, I slay me! I'm only kidding. You should've seen your faces!" He lowered his head until his snout almost touched their heads—and sniffed them, like Grucinda had done. What was it with everyone smelling them? Sure, they'd been running and sweating, but she didn't think they stank *that* bad.

"Wait," the beast said. "Are you two children? Like, human?"

"Y-yeah," Julián stammered.

"I've never met real human children before. Are you tasty?"

Valentina froze. Julián's breath came out in short bursts.

The dragon dissolved in a fit of laughter again. "Ha! Kidding again!"

Valentina's legs buckled beneath her, and she sank onto the wet earth. Papi's stories had apparently failed to mention the monster was a comedian. Her heart still hammered, but she was pretty sure he wouldn't eat them.

"How did you get past the enchantments?" the dragon asked.

Valentina found her voice. "We don't know. And neither does Grucinda." She relayed how they found the tunnel after the earthquake and landed in Tierra de los Olvidados, with Julián interjecting every so often. Remembering Papi renewed her resolve. She stood up and dusted herself.

"Wowzer," the dragon said. "No one's ever tricked the portal before."

"We didn't trick it," Valentina said crossly. How could they trick a portal they didn't even know existed? None of it made sense, but it didn't matter. The only thing that mattered at the moment was getting to Madremonte and saving Papi.

Julián stepped closer to the dragon, studying him with intense fascination. Her brother's fear seemed to have disappeared.

"What's your name?" Julián asked.

"Oh, where are my manners? I'm Albetroz, Dragon of the River." He lowered his head as if in a small bow.

"I'm Julián. This is my sister, Vale." He reached out a hand and hesitated. "Can I pet you? I've always wanted to meet a real dragon."

"Sure!" Albetroz grinned, showing four rows of sharp teeth.

Valentina cringed. If the dragon was trying to look friendly, it wasn't working. Julián didn't seem to mind though. He rubbed Albetroz's side, then scratched behind his ears, causing the dragon to growl and slap his tail on the water.

Maybe he's part dog, Valentina thought, before telling her brother, "Okay, ya, basta."

But Julián poked Albetroz's scaly wings, sending him into a fit of laughter. "That tickles!"

"Stop touching the dragon," Valentina snapped. There was a phrase she never thought she'd say. "We need to keep going, remember?"

Julián sobered and dropped his arms.

Satisfied, Valentina turned to Albetroz. "Grucinda said you could help us get to Madremonte's castle so we can save our dad. The patasola came to Grucinda's house before she could tell us more, and we think the brujita's in trouble."

Albetroz's playfulness vanished. The air around them thickened and his eyes darkened. "HOW DARE SHE!" the dragon thundered, and Valentina shrank back. Then he shook his head and said sheepishly, "Sorry. I forgot myself. Patasola blames Grucinda for Marcos's disappearance, but she can't prove it, and that drives her loca."

"Who's Marcos?" Valentina asked.

"Oh." Albetroz puckered his snout. "Maybe I shouldn't have said that. Grucinda wouldn't be happy."

"She's not here," Julián pointed out.

"Right." Albetroz bobbed his head to some silent rhythm. "Marcos is Madremonte's lost son. He's been missing since the time of La Gran Violencia."

Valentina processed what the dragon said. The queen's guard blamed the brujita for the prince's disappearance. Could Grucinda really have had a hand in it? Valentina's gut told her no, that the brujita was innocent. Besides, Madremonte would've probably had her imprisoned—or worse—if it were true. Unless Grucinda had tricked everyone and meddled with the portal. That might explain how they got through, though it didn't explain why she had helped them.

"What happened to him?" Julián asked.

Albetroz shook his head. "No one knows. Some say Marcos was murdered. Others say he was kidnapped. Most say humans did it, and the patasola says Grucinda helped. All I know is there are many chismes getting tangled and hiding the truth, like my abuela used to say."

"That's so sad," Valentina said. And it was, but they needed to keep moving. "We could really use your help. We need to reach the Bosque de Sueños and head to Madremonte's castle. She's the only way home to save our father."

"Say no more! A friend of Grucinda's is a friend of mine," Albetroz said. "Climb on."

"Wait, what?" Valentina sputtered, just as Julián exclaimed, "Cool!"

She'd thought the dragon would point them in the right

direction and help them cross the river. She wasn't exactly prepared to ride him.

"Climb on my back," Albetroz insisted, lowering his wings. Julián didn't need more prompting. He climbed over them and onto the dragon's back. Valentina hesitated. They needed to go, but could they truly trust him?

"I'll zip you through the river to the Bosque de Sueños, and then you'll be at Madremonte's castle in about two or three days. It'll be longer if you try to cross the plains on foot."

"My dad doesn't have two or three days!" Valentina's voice hitched. It hadn't looked so far on Grucinda's map.

"Fear not," Albetroz said. "I can swim faster than fast—even faster than a speeding sailfish!" He swayed as if readying for a race. "It'll take us only a couple hours to get to the forest. That'll save you *at least* a day and a half. Besides, time crawls much slower in the human world. That's what Grucinda always says, anyway."

"Wouldn't flying to the castle be faster?" Riding Albetroz through the air sounded just as terrifying, but if she had to ride him at all, then she might as well take the fastest route.

"I'm afraid not," Albetroz said.

"But you have wings!" she said.

"Alas, my wings are not suited for flight. They let me race beneath the water, though. And they're fashionable." He raised his wings, striking a pose. Then he said sadly, "My kind used to be able to fly, before the border shut. I don't know what that's like."

"Vale," Julián groaned. "You're wasting time! Just get on." He had positioned himself behind one of Albetroz's fins and looked ready for an adventure.

Valentina swallowed hard. The Forest of Dreams was exactly

where Grucinda had told them to go on their way to the mountains. If riding the dragon was the fastest way to the queen, then so be it.

She climbed onto Albetroz's outstretched wing and held on for dear life as the diablo ballena took off down the river, leaving the bamboo forest and Grucinda behind them.

TWELVE

Riding a mythical dragon was much like riding a wild horse—unpredictable at best, and you had to hold on or you'd be thrown off and trampled.

Valentina gripped Albetroz's fins for dear life as he raced down the river, taking curves without pausing. She bumped along, feeling her fingers slipping, and she imagined the worst: sliding down lengths of leathery scales before getting lashed by a slithering tail and drowning.

She grunted, repositioning her grip.

Julián, on the other hand, hooted with joy.

Water whipped around them, tugging the hair loose from her ponytail. She gritted her teeth and squeezed her eyes shut, praying for the ride to end.

The longer they tore through the river, though, the more she felt her worry wash away. She opened her eyes and a giggle slipped from her lips.

As if inspired by her sudden shift, Albetroz leaped out of the water and then dove in. Valentina shrieked, sure they were going to drown, but somehow, water surrounded them without touching them. It was as if they'd been wrapped in an airtight magical bubble. Valentina watched in wonder as the current flew by, a show of light and sparkle and movement. Schools of fish scattered out of their way, their scales twinkling like starlight in the colorful water.

Valentina squealed in delight as they moved deeper into Tierra de los Olvidados and toward the Bosque de Sueños. She leaned into Albetroz. Everything felt possible on the back of a dragon slicing through the river.

After a while, Albetroz slowed, and they resurfaced. The landscape to her left still reminded Valentina of the Llanos Orientales—grass, grass, and more marshy grass—but now she saw a cluster of treetops lining the river on her right.

"Who knew you could still have fun?" Julián said to Valentina.

She rolled her eyes, then asked Albetroz, "Is that the Forest of Dreams?"

"Yup!" the dragon said.

That was the forest they'd have to cross, and just beyond that, they'd find the Cordillera Monumental. Valentina tried to make out the smudged peaks in the distance.

Albetroz's tail propelled them forward. A few critters scattered from shore before Valentina could get a good look at them. Suddenly, she had an uneasy foreboding. They were too visible on Albetroz's back. Anyone could spot them and alert the queen and her guard. If the patasola caught them before they reached the queen, they'd die.

That couldn't happen. They needed to stay alive if they wanted to help Papi.

Another thought crossed her mind. "Grucinda said we'll find Madremonte's castle and her portal in the mountains," she told the dragon. "But we don't even know what the portal looks like or where it is."

"Ooh! Ooh! I know," Albetroz said, raising his wing. "It's in her ring."

"Why would anyone put a portal in a ring?" Julián asked.

Albetroz shrugged, his wings grazing against their legs.

"Madremonte wants the only live connection to the human world on her at all times. I think she still hopes that one day, Marcos will return, and this way she'll be the first to see him."

Valentina felt a pang of sadness for the queen. "What does the ring look like?"

"It's an emerald encased in gold."

"Emerald and gold," Valentina repeated. "That's so weird. Colombia's famous for both. We have whole museos for them."

Albetroz snorted. "Why would anyone put gems and metals in museums? They belong to the earth."

Valentina had never thought about it that way.

The Bosque de Sueños grew larger as they approached, and Valentina couldn't help but wonder which of the Colombian forests this one would resemble. Would it be more like the Andean ones, or the Pacific ones? Would it be like those in the Llanos, with woods interrupting marshes?

"Why is this land called Tierra de los Olvidados?" she asked suddenly.

Albetroz dipped his head into the river and emerged moments later with a fish flapping in his mouth. He slurped it up, spit out the bones, and said, "Isn't it awful? That wasn't always our name. We were once Tierra de Paz."

"You went from being Land of Peace to Land of the Forgotten?" Julián leaned in, settling himself more comfortably on the dragon's back. "They're not even close."

"Uh-huh. That was long, long ago. Before I was born. Grucinda tells me the story often." Albetroz's voice turned wistful. "She says those days were full of peace, when humans and our kind came and went from each other's worlds, and we traded without fear. I always wanted to meet humans."

"That sounds awesome," Valentina said, imagining what it

might've been like growing up spending summers here, without fear of getting caught and disposed of.

"Right?" Albetroz said. "Imagínate—we could've already met! We could've had swim meets and land-and-sea races. I could've terrorized humans and sent them screaming down mountainsides." He let out a wistful sigh.

"There's already stories of that happening in our world," Julián said.

"Huh. That was probably my bisabuela. She had all the fun."

Valentina shook her head, chuckling. There wasn't just one diablo ballena but a whole family of them! "What changed?"

"Humans got too violent, and that violence spilled into our land. They were destroying their world and ours. For a while, Madremonte tried to protect everyone with her magic, but everything changed when her son disappeared. The official story is that a pair of humans took him, but no one could find him, even though she sent legions to search both worlds. She closed the borders and locked us away, and with that, the land renamed itself."

"That's awful," Valentina said.

"Yep," the dragon agreed. "Our world has never been the same."

They'd slowed even more and were approaching the riverbank beside the Bosque de Sueños. Despite the need to keep going, Valentina didn't want to say goodbye to Albetroz yet. She had grown to like this silly dragon.

"How old was Marcos?" Julián asked.

"Only five," Albetroz said sadly. "It broke our queen and punished all of us."

"What do you mean?" Valentina asked.

"Our borders have been closed for hundreds of years, and your world is forgetting us. If no one remembers, we become endangered."

Endangered. Valentina remembered Señora Uribe's science lessons about the many animals in Colombia that were vanishing because humans hunted them or because their natural habitats or food sources were destroyed, like the Colombian weasel. "What happens if everyone forgets?"

Albetroz stopped at the edge of the forest and spread his wings so Valentina and Julián could hop down. "We stop existing."

Valentina's legs felt like jelly as she gripped the scales and made her way onto the dusty earth. Julián slipped down after.

"Our Papi writes your stories down," Julián said. "His dad told them to him, and now he makes it his job to tell everyone about you. He won't let anyone forget."

"Neither will we," Valentina said, surprised by her own conviction.

"You better not," Albetroz thundered. "Or I'll find a way to haunt your dreams."

Valentina cringed.

"Just kidding!" Albetroz roared. When he stopped laughing, he said, "Who knew I would get to meet a pair of human children in my lifetime?" He splashed them with his slithering tail.

"Hey!" Valentina shrieked, then dissolved into giggles.

Soon, though, she sobered. If humans had taken Madremonte's son, how in the world would she and Julián live long enough to convince her they were different? Maybe the sight of two children trying to make their way back to their father would stir the queen's sympathy.

Maybe. But suddenly, the chances of that happening felt impossible.

THIRTEEN

They said goodbye to Albetroz too soon. Before he left, he warned: "Serious talk. Not everyone's a friend. Be careful and stay as hidden as possible."

Valentina nodded. The memory of the patasola barging into Grucinda's cottage left a sour taste in her mouth. Then, thinking of the trek ahead, she asked, "Do you know if the water is safe to drink?" Grucinda had given them enough food to last awhile, but once their canteens ran out, they'd need to find more water. They wouldn't survive the trek to the madremonte's castle without it.

"You can drink the water of rivers and lakes just fine," Albetroz said. "Everything on our land is edible and drinkable, even for humans."

Valentina made a mental note of that.

"Will we see you again?" Julián asked.

"Maybe if you come back this way. I can only move in the deeper rivers, and the ones by the mountains are shallower. I've gotten stuck a time or two." He chuckled.

Valentina felt a pang of sadness as he dove into the water and, with a final splash, swam away. "You know," she said after a bit, "I never imagined all this being real. The brujita's cottage. The patasola. The diablo ballena. I mean, I know Papi *said* it all existed, but . . ." She trailed off, shaking her head.

"That's 'cause your head's always stuck in a notebook. For being an artist, you have a terrible imagination," Julián said. "I always knew they existed."

Valentina struggled to give flight to the words fluttering in her chest. Night after night in the finca, she and her brother would listen to Papi's stories. But those were two-dimensional to her, like charcoal stick figures. This—Albetroz, Grucinda, the cottage, the grotto back in the tunnel—this was a master's three-dimensional portrait come to life.

"I need this magic when we get home," Julián said. "Mami would never have to bug me to clean my room. All I'd have to do is snap and—poof! Clean."

Valentina giggled. "Yeah, life would be so much easier with magic in it." Then, another thought occurred to her. Could magic heal the earth back home, the restless volcanoes, the earthquakes and droughts? Maybe the reopening of the border would help *both* worlds—it would keep the beings of Tierra de los Olvidados from extinction and it would restore the land in Colombia. If that were true, Valentina would have to convince Madremonte that it was worth keeping the connection between worlds open.

Right. Because convincing her to help save Papi isn't enough, Valentina thought dryly.

Above them, the sun inched toward its resting spot, splattering the sky in shades of rose gold and plum. Heat bore down, and a line of sweat gathered on Valentina's brows. Shadows in the grove of trees lengthened, making the Bosque de Sueños look like anything but a dream.

As if reading her mind, Julián asked, "We're supposed to go in there?"

Between the riverbank and the forest, a trail of tall grass led to a small lagoon a short distance away. If only they could stay out here and not have to trudge into a dark forest.

"Yeah," Valentina said. "We go through the forest until we reach the mountains. Then climb until we reach the queen's castle. But how do we know we're going in the right direction?"

"Um, we have a map," Julián pointed out.

Valentina scowled and dug through her mochila until she found the witch's parchment. She spread it open and stared at the squiggles and lines representing the mountains, forests, and rivers. She studied the corner with the brujita's cottage and felt a pang of uneasiness. She hoped Grucinda was okay, wherever the patasola had taken her.

The more she looked at the map, the more she realized with certainty that Tierra de los Olvidados was a mirror image of Colombia. Instead of being on the east side of the map, like the Andes, the Cordillera Monumental was on the west. El Desierto de Oro lay on the southwest corner, near Grucinda's cottage, while la Guajira in Colombia was on the northeast. The Llanos Orientales and Llanos Orgullosos? Flipped. Two oceans bordered Tierra de los Olvidados on the east and west, like bookends. Colombia, too, was surrounded by two bodies of water: the Caribbean Sea to the north and the Pacific Ocean to the west. The only thing that seemed to be in the same spot as back home was a rainforest in the southeast corner of the map.

What did it mean that their worlds shared so much in common?

"Vale, look." Julián pointed at a spot on the map.

"What?" Valentina peered closer. There on the parchment were the letters *V* and *J*. "Oh!"

"That's us!" Julián said.

Valentina moved with the map in her hands, and sure enough, the small *V* shifted place. "Increíble. This is perfect! As long as we have the map, we'll know exactly where we're going. We just need to stay focused and check often. We can figure out what we'll say to Madremonte on the way."

They had a plan. Sort of. It was good enough for now.

"Can we at least eat something before we go into the forest of doom?" Julián asked.

Valentina hesitated, but when her stomach grumbled, she said, "Fine. But once we go in, I don't want to stop."

They sat against a large boulder near the riverbank, and Valentina dug through her mochila for the bread and cheese Grucinda had given them. She took a swig from her canteen, feeling the cool water soothe her parched tongue. Julián, too, unwrapped his food.

They ate quickly. When she'd eaten a quarter of the food, Valentina wrapped it back in the towel. Even though Albetroz said that everything on this land was edible, the responsible thing was to ration what they had. Mami would be proud of her.

Valentina's heart wrinkled, thinking about Mami. Was she worried about them? Had she tried calling Papi? "Vamos," she said, standing up. "We have to keep going."

"But I'm still hungry," Julián said.

"We can't eat it all now. We have to be smart and make it last."

Valentina helped him up, and they collected their belongings. Ahead of them, the grass rustled. Was it the wind? Couldn't be. There was no breeze, nothing to wick away her sweat. She heard it again. Swish. Swish. Swish.

"There's something there," she whispered, pointing at the spot.

"I don't see anything."

Valentina frowned, staring in concentration. She heard a slithering sound, like something being dragged. Goose bumps rose on her arms and neck. When Julián looked over at her, she put her finger against her lips. As she watched, the patch of grass rustled again.

Her brother stepped closer to her. "What do you think it is?"

They were in a magical world with legendary creatures. It could be anything—from a rat to a beast the size of Albetroz. Though Valentina doubted it would be something as large as the dragon. They'd have seen it already looming above the grass.

"I don't know," she whispered back. "A snake?"

She really hoped it wasn't. She hated snakes. Cautiously, she stepped forward, Julián close behind her.

"There!" she said.

A furry creature passed within a few feet from them. It resembled a crab, only with long, matted fur, and it scuttled between the tall blades on several legs, bobbing as if it couldn't keep its balance. It dragged the remains of a dead snake.

Julián sucked in a breath.

"What *is* that?" Valentina murmured.

The creature stopped. One of its paws rose in the air like a tentacle and Valentina realized with shock that they weren't paws at all. They were fingers, covered with thick, knotted brown hair and tipped with lethally sharp nails. The more she stared, the more Valentina realized the creature had the shape of a hand that had been chopped off at the wrist. Two beady eyes glared at them from between the knuckles.

Julián squeezed her arm so hard she was sure he left a mark. Valentina didn't have to be a mind reader to know that her brother recognized this creature from Papi's legends.

The mano peluda.

The legend of the hairy hand was one parents told their children to scare them into behaving—or one older cousins and siblings told the younger ones to freak them out. It was said to live under beds, waiting to wrap around kids' ankles and drag them into the void. Valentina had always scoffed at those stories.

Suddenly, the mano peluda dropped the snake and bared its fangs, hidden beneath two fingernails. "Intruders!" it shrieked.

FOURTEEN

Valentina stumbled back. Beside her, Julián said, "Can we outrun it?"

"INTRUDERS," the mano peluda bellowed again, louder this time.

"Shhh," Valentina pleaded, palms up and voice soft, as one would do with a wounded animal. "We're not here to hurt you."

In response, the creature emitted a third shrill shriek and charged at them. It would have been laughable had it not moved so quickly.

"Run!" Valentina yelled.

For the second time that day, she and her brother ran. Her breath came in short puffs as she zigzagged through the grass, her mochila bumping against her back, the package with their provisions clutched against her chest.

"Do you think it can swim?" Julián called as the lagoon came into full view.

The hairy hand closed in on them, the swish, swish, swish of the rustling grass alerting them to its nearness.

"I don't know!"

Valentina couldn't think. Her legs ached. Her chest hurt. It was hot and muggy—this was way worse than trekking through the Andes in search of the patasola.

Her brother darted straight into the lagoon.

"¿Estás loco?" Valentina cried. But when the hairy hand clawed the space near her feet, she splashed in after him.

The mano peluda stood at the edge of the water, hissing and yapping. Valentina shuddered at the thought of the claws coming near her skin. She didn't want to find out if they were poisonous, like some of the legends claimed.

"Who's crazy now?" Julián panted.

"Whatever." Valentina's chest heaved. "We can't stay here."

She eyed the disembodied hand. Every time she shifted toward one end of the pond, it followed on dry ground. When she changed course, it did too, like a wolf trapping its prey.

"But how do we get out?" Julián asked. "That thing's worse than an attack dog."

They'd never cross the forest or reach the queen if they stayed stuck here in the lagoon because of the stupid mano peluda.

"Scat!" Julián screamed. "Go away!" He hit the surface of the water with an open palm, splashing the creature.

It didn't budge, only shook itself thoroughly before baring its fangs again.

Valentina groaned. "It's not a cat."

They were trapped, and the sun dipped lower into the forest ahead. If they didn't get out of here, Madremonte's guard would get them. The patasola had probably already heard the creature's cries and was on the way.

They had to get out. They had to reach the forest. There, they could hide.

"I'm sorry," she told the creature. It hissed back. "You're not giving us another choice."

Valentina cringed, hating what she was about to do. Without thinking about it more, she slipped off her mochila and swung it at the mano peluda. It struck with a sickening thump. The creature soared through the air and landed with a yelp.

Valentina stared at the spot between tall blades of grass, feeling queasy. Was it okay? She hadn't wanted to hurt it, only stun it. With growing uneasiness, she realized this would not look good. The creatures in Tierra de los Olvidados already thought all humans were violent and cruel, and what she'd just done proved them right.

Had Valentina ruined their chances with the queen?

"Vamos." Julián tugged on her arm, pulling her out of the lagoon. "We have to go before it wakes up."

Her wet clothes stuck to her skin, though in the afternoon heat, it felt refreshing. She slipped on her mochila and started to follow her brother when she realized their food, which she'd been clutching as they ran, was gone. She'd dropped it in the lagoon.

"Our food!" she moaned. "What are we going to eat now?" A wave of worry overwhelmed her. They needed strength for their journey ahead.

"Albetroz said we can eat from the land," Julián said.

"But what can we find in there?" She pointed at the forest.

Julián shrugged. "We'll figure it out."

Somewhere in the distance, a wail pierced the silence, long and deep and mournful. Valentina didn't know if it belonged to an animal or a mythical creature, and she didn't want to find out. Her skin prickled, as had happened before the earthquake. She waited for the inevitable worsening of symptoms, for the earth to start rolling.

Nothing happened.

Her breathing evened, and soon, she sighed in relief. She couldn't deal with another earthquake. Not now.

Julián sniffed the air. "Does that smell like—?"

"Food." She stared at her brother. The unmistakable scent of roasting fish lingered in the air. Could they be that lucky? Was this a trick?

Julián darted alongside the trees, staying parallel to the lagoon, which branched out into a babbling creek. Valentina followed close behind. He stopped beside a mound of dirt, which rose on an incline. Nestled within it was a door made from weathered tree trunks. It was large enough for Valentina to duck through if it were open.

"What is that?" she said.

"Someone's house?" Julián offered.

The scent of food was stronger here. Someone was cooking in there, and Valentina's stomach grumbled in response.

"Look." Julián stood beside a small window in the dirt.

Valentina peered in. "Whoa." A soft glow illuminated a narrow passageway that dipped downward and spilled into a wide chamber. In one corner stood an iron stove, fire crackling within it. In the middle, two animals sat at a long table, roughly carved from oaks. She recognized the giant gray armadillo, which in Colombia was endangered, from Señora Uribe's science lessons, but the other she didn't. It reminded her of an oversized guinea pig with a thick body, four squat legs, and a flat, hairy snout.

"This must be some kind of burrow," Valentina said softly. But burrows brought to mind long tunnels burrowed into the earth. Not a home with a working stove.

"Do you think we can ask them for food?" Julián asked.

Valentina shook her head. "Too dangerous. Besides—" She peered inside again. "We don't know if they're friendly."

Julián chewed on the insides of his cheeks. "What if one of us tricks them to come out and the other runs in and grabs food?"

"You don't even know what they're eating. Don't armadillos eat bugs and termites?"

"I'd eat ants at this point, I'm so hungry!"

Valentina pressed her lips together. A small breeze hit her wet clothes, making her shiver. The temperature was dropping quickly. Warmth and food sounded wonderful, especially before they moved on. "I guess it could work."

Just then, a low growl from behind made them spin around, and they came face-to-face with a large spotted ocelot, who stalked toward them. "What do we have here?"

FIFTEEN

They should've kept going. They could've found food somewhere else. Why had she followed her brother?

"We don't mean any harm," Valentina said. "We were hungry, and—"

"So you thought to steal from my friends?" the ocelot snarled.

"What? No!" Valentina said. "Barter." Mami would kill them if they stole anything. When Valentina was seven, she'd made the mistake of slipping some candy into her pockets at the mercado. When Mami found out, she dragged Valentina all the way back and forced her to pay not just the price of the candy but also a fine.

Valentina learned her lesson. If they'd gone in and snuck food, she would've left something of theirs as payment. A drawing. Or maybe her favorite pencils.

"Please," Valentina said. "We're hungry."

"And we have a long journey," Julián added.

"Likely story from a pair of humans. I thought your kind had been exterminated from our land." The ocelot scowled. This close, its orange fur looked almost neon, speckled with black spots. Though it barely reached Valentina's shoulders, its sharp teeth held an unspoken threat.

The door beside them swung open. Golden light stretched out from the opening as the giant armadillo ambled out, snout twitching. Its scales, which wrapped around its body and head like armor, shimmered a silvery gray.

"Oh dear," it said. "What's this, Don Babou?"

"I caught some trespassers, Don Pedro," the ocelot said.

"Is that Don Babou?" came a gravelly voice from within the burrow. "He's late!" The oversized guinea pig waddled out of the opening and stopped short when its gaze landed on Valentina and Julián. Tan shaggy hair covered its body, and up close, it was as tall as Julián. "Were we having more guests?"

The armadillo, Don Pedro, inclined his head. "It appears so, Doña Ruth."

"These aren't guests," the ocelot spat. "They're filthy humans!"

I resent that, Valentina thought, but she decided to keep quiet. She didn't want to give Don Babou any reason to attack them.

"Oh my!" Doña Ruth released a few short barks.

"Now, now," said Don Pedro. "Let's go back inside and see if we can't sort this out. You don't want to be talking about *humans* out in plain sight." He glanced furtively around before turning back into his burrow. Doña Ruth huffed but followed behind him, leaving Valentina and Julián alone with Don Babou.

"We really weren't trying to steal," Valentina said meekly.

Don Babou growled, "If it weren't for Don Pedro, I would've eaten you already. Go on. Any funny moves, and I'll end you right here."

They marched into the burrow with an angry ocelot at their back.

Though it had looked larger from outside, the interior of the den felt welcoming. Warmth radiated from the iron stove, which held a roasting fish within its fire. The scent prompted a painful pang in Valentina's stomach.

Don Babou pushed them forward. Julián stumbled, and Valentina reached out, pulling him close to her. He wiggled out of her grasp.

"I'm fine," he grumbled.

"So what're we going to do with them?" Don Babou said.

"Why, welcome them to our table," said Don Pedro, closing the door. "They are mere children."

The wild cat slunk toward a corner. "They're human and they planned to steal from you. Treachery, I tell you!"

Doña Ruth stood beside Don Pedro, effectively blocking Valentina and Julián's only exit. The walls of the burrow narrowed. Valentina's heartbeat drummed in her ears. She glanced around wildly, trying to find another way out.

There wasn't.

"What *I'd* like to know," said Doña Ruth, "is how a pair of humans, children no less, could have crossed the border."

"Indeed," Don Pedro said. "I am quite curious to hear how you came to be in our land. It has been too long since we've seen your kind."

"They're a threat," Don Babou repeated. "They need to be disposed of."

"No, no disposing of us, please!" Valentina said quickly. What could she tell them to calm them down?

Before she could make up her mind, Julián said defiantly, "We need to see Madremonte. We're hungry. We've been traveling all day and your food smelled delicious."

Valentina glanced at the kind, gentle eyes of Don Pedro, so different from the glaring gaze of Don Babou and the hostile scowl of Doña Ruth. "Our father was hurt," she added. "I'm not sure how we got here, but we need Madremonte's help to get back and save him."

"You believe our queen will offer aid?" Don Pedro asked.

"I hope so," Valentina said. "She's our only way back home. I can give you something in return for some food. I don't have much, but maybe this will do."

Valentina rummaged through her mochila, finding the only thing of value she carried: her sketch pad. She flipped through her drawings, finding one of dawn cresting the Andes at her family's finca. It was one of her favorites, showing golden light bathing the mountains in a way that looked otherworldly. Like magic. It was the first drawing of her portfolio. But there would be no Bogotá Academy of Arts next year if they couldn't reach the queen and save Papi. Before she could change her mind, she tore the sheet from the pad and handed it to Don Pedro.

The giant armadillo grasped it with his claws. "You made this? It's quite lovely."

Valentina nodded, warmth creeping into her cheeks. "Gracias."

Don Babou looked between her and the armadillo, shaking his head. "You're a fool, Don Pedro," he said. "You're too kind for your own good. But I won't get caught up in a web of disloyalty. See that the queen doesn't find out you've helped a human."

And with that, he stalked out into the night, slamming the door behind him.

SIXTEEN

Don Pedro gave a little shrug. "Don't mind him. He's suffered greatly at the hands of humans."

"What happened?" Julián asked.

Doña Ruth answered, "Most of his family was slaughtered for their fur."

Valentina gasped. "That's horrible!"

"Yes, well, humans have done some atrocious things in our land." Doña Ruth sniffed.

"I'm sorry," Valentina said. She felt a pang of guilt, even though it wasn't her fault other people were awful. She thought about the violence that had plagued Colombia throughout its history and the damage people were doing right now, destroying the land to build more and not caring how it affected the animals living on it. People sucked sometimes.

"Hasn't the border been closed for hundreds of years?" Julián asked. "How old *is* he?"

Don Pedro chuckled. "Our kind live quite a long time, some even thousands of years. Don Babou was merely a cub when the border closed. He's almost four hundred now."

"How's that even possible?" Valentina asked.

"Time is a curious thing. In our world, the balance between earth and creature creates a kind of paradise that elongates the passage of time, not as in your world. In some ways, it is why our queen decided to close the border, to preserve our people from the dangers of the human world." Silence hung around the room, like a heavy cloak. "But come," Don Pedro said, making his way toward the stove. "Enough talk of the past. Warm up and have some food."

"We can't stay too long," Valentina said, following the armadillo, "but it would be awesome to have some warm food to get us through the forest."

Don Pedro pointed to the chairs nearest the stove. "Sit by the hearth so your clothes dry, too. Go on."

Julián plopped into his seat. Valentina felt less certain, but she sat beside her brother and watched as the armadillo ambled toward shelves near the stove. From her vantage point, she saw jars filled with nuts and fruits on the topmost one, while bowls of insects sat on the bottom one, each labeled neatly. She gagged at the thought of eating ants, termites, and beetles, no matter how well seasoned they might be.

Doña Ruth scowled at them before waddling over to Don Pedro. The two spoke in hushed tones as they prepared the fish and filled bowls with nuts and fruits.

Valentina frowned. Every moment felt wasted. She was grateful for the meal, but she wished the armadillo would hurry. She shifted, about to get up and offer help, when she heard Doña Ruth say, "Madremonte won't like this."

Valentina leaned back, trying to hear better.

"They're harmless, poor things," Don Pedro said.

"That's neither here nor there. Our queen has forbidden it," Doña Ruth whispered. "If she knows we helped them, it's the garrison for us."

"Perhaps. But they bring the possibility of change, my dear. Things have not been the same since young Marcos went missing. It would do Madremonte good to remember not all humans are like those who took her son."

Yeah, we're not! Valentina thought indignantly. But she couldn't blame Madremonte for thinking otherwise.

"How are you sure they can be trusted?" Doña Ruth asked.

"Because I can smell it on them." Then Don Pedro turned, staring right at Valentina. "Though eavesdropping is highly impolite."

Valentina flushed. "Perdón," she said, straightening in her chair. "I just . . ." She trailed off before she dug herself in deeper. "I'm sorry."

"Apology accepted," Don Pedro said.

"Hmph," Doña Ruth said.

Valentina glared. Clearly, this oversized guinea pig didn't want them there. Why couldn't she have left, like Don Babou had? Don Pedro balanced the tray with the bowls and set it at the table. Doña Ruth brought over a jug of juice.

"What kind of animal are you?" Julián asked her.

Doña Ruth's expression soured further. "How rude."

She reminded Valentina of their tía Dolores. Anytime Valentina's family visited her in Bogotá, her great-aunt moaned about Vale and her brother—though mostly about Julián. According to her, they were uncivilized terremotos who had no manners. Valentina bit back a laugh, imagining her tía abuela as a giant rodent.

"If you must know," Doña Ruth said finally, "I'm a capybara."

Valentina had never seen a capybara in person, only in Mami's documentaries. But Doña Ruth was much larger than those other capybaras had looked on screen.

"Cálmate, querida," Don Pedro told her. "There is no point in getting your fur in a tangle." He chuckled before nudging two bowls full of fish and moras toward Valentina and Julián. "I suppose Don Babou won't be eating with us after all, and perhaps you might need this more at the moment."

"Yes!" Julián shoved a spoonful into his mouth. "Fank ou."

Valentina glared at her brother, who shrugged. Deep-purple juice dribbled out of the corners of his mouth. Shaking her head, she scooped up some of the fish and berries. They were remarkably tasty.

"So how *did* you come to be here?" Doña Ruth asked, her webbed paws tapping on the table.

Valentina set her spoon down. She thought about lying and making up some story, but she was too tired to think through an elaborate tale. So, she settled on a brief version of the truth. She told them about the earthquake and their father getting trapped and falling down the mountain. "We got stuck inside a tunnel that brought us here," she finished.

Julián added, "And Grucinda told us where to go."

Valentina kicked her brother under the table. He lifted his shoulders, as if saying, "What?" She hadn't planned on mentioning the brujita, though if Grucinda had been taken prisoner, then it didn't matter.

Doña Ruth said, "Is that so?"

"Yes," Valentina said. "If we don't get back, our father will die."

"Oh, dear," Don Pedro said. "I do hope you can convince our queen. Perhaps . . ." He paused. "While I must stay here, Doña Ruth could accompany you through the forest tomorrow."

"Excuse me?" Doña Ruth squeaked.

"Tomorrow?" Valentina shook her head. "No, we can't waste more time."

"If I may." Don Pedro leaned forward, both clawed paws gripping the table. "It's evening, and the Bosque de Sueños is much more amiable during the day. Perhaps it might be best for you to sleep now and continue at dawn." Then, to Doña Ruth, he added, "The children will have a greater chance of reaching their destination unharmed if we help them. I would go myself, but I'm afraid my eyesight is quite poor to navigate the Bosque."

The last thing Valentina wanted was a sour capybara following them. She didn't trust Doña Ruth, and it was clear the feeling was mutual.

"What's in the forest?" Julián asked. "El silbón? El sombrerón? El cura sin cabeza? Wait, are there wild predators? I've always wanted to see a jaguar or a bear up close."

Doña Ruth huffed. "All sorts of trickster beings and animals are in there. If you ask me, it's nothing but trouble. Forest of Dreams—ha! More like Forest of Nightmares."

Where did you send us, Grucinda? Valentina thought.

Maybe they could sleep a few hours and be up before dawn. They *would* need all their strength to trek the rest of the way. With food and rest, they could walk twice as fast and make up for any lost time. Besides, time was supposed to move slower in the human world than it did here.

"I guess it won't hurt," she said finally. "But I really don't want to bother Doña Ruth."

"No bother at all," the armadillo answered for the capybara, who looked as uncomfortable as an anteater whose snout had gotten stuck in an anthill.

Julián said quietly, "We'd get through the forest faster with her."

This was true. And, *if* the capybara could be trusted, they'd also lessen their chances of getting lost. They had the map, but a guide would make the trip less stressful.

Valentina sighed. "Fine."

After their meal, Don Pedro excused himself for the night, promising to see them off in the morning. Doña Ruth curled up beside the stove. An uneasy current wiggled in Valentina's belly.

She leaned back on the soft earth and stared at the burrow's ceiling. Though her body ached, she couldn't fall asleep. Her mind was restless. Beside her, Julián snored softly.

She turned on her side, slipped off the locket hanging around her neck, and unclasped it. In the remaining glow of the fire, she studied her parents' faces. Mami was about three and held her chin up, staring defiantly at the camera. Papi was older in his photo. Five? Six? His gaze held the same mischievous twinkle as Julián's. In fact, Papi, Julián, and Abuelito all had looked almost identical as little kids: thick brown hair, wide hazel eyes with thick lashes, a strong nose, and a contagious grin. Now Julián looked more like Mami, though his piercing gaze was still all Papi.

"We're coming," Valentina whispered, imagining the wind taking her words across their worlds to her father.

When she was five, Valentina had snuck out of the finca and made her way to the pond with the geese. Somehow, she managed to open the gate, only to discover that geese were fiercely protective of their territory. They attacked and she ran blindly, tumbling into the pond. She remembered the dark water surrounding her and her body sinking. Just before she lost consciousness, strong arms pulled her out. Papi had seen her falling in from his cottage studio and raced to save her. "You're okay, mi chiquitica," he'd said over and over. "You're safe. Papi's got you."

Now she sat up, wiping the wetness from her face. She would save him the way he'd saved her. That was a promise.

In the distance, thunder rumbled, and she felt the echo of it in her chest. *The earth is not happy.* She waited for the nausea and dizziness to hit, but like earlier, nothing happened. She couldn't shake the feeling there was something *more* to these feelings. But what?

With a sigh, she pulled her mochila toward her, sifting through it until she found her sketch pad. If she couldn't sleep, she might as well draw. When this was all over, she had a portfolio to submit. She found a blank page and let the events of the day wash over her: the earthquake, the cave and grotto, Grucinda's cottage, riding Albetroz through the river, Don Pedro's burrow. Every detail of this mystical and confounding day spilled from her fingers as she drew.

After a while, it started drizzling outside. She stashed her sketch pad and lay back down, listening to the falling rain. It was a song, beautiful and haunting.

Somewhere in the distance, a lonesome wail echoed across the sky.

SEVENTEEN

Valentina awoke shivering. Something cold and wet pooled around her feet. Groggily, she opened her eyes and stretched—and her hands splashed water.

She shrieked, scrambling up and snatching her mochila just before it got completely soaked. All sleepiness evaporated. With a sinking feeling, she found the source: water gurgled into Don Pedro's burrow under the front door and collected on the ground where she'd been sleeping.

Valentina darted outside. The sky wept in an endless sea of darkness. From where she stood, she couldn't even see the Bosque de Sueños or the Río de Mil Colores. She could, however, hear the roar of the river.

She raced back inside. "Julián! Doña Ruth! Don Pedro! Get up! We have to get out!" She shook her brother, who grumbled and flipped onto his belly. His face landed in a puddle and he sprung up, blinking hard.

"What the heck?" he said.

Rain thundered on the dirt roof, snatching their words.

"The river's flooding," she yelled back.

Doña Ruth was fully awake beside them now. "Oh my stars. We must get Don Pedro." She waddled past a bamboo partition in the rear of the burrow.

"Don Pedro!" Julián called, running after the capybara. "The river!"

Behind the partition, the burrow was narrower than the space where Valentina, Julián, and Doña Ruth had slept. Two small windows opened toward the outdoors, where the rain pelted the ground. Don Pedro scurried back and forth with two pails, trying to scoop water out the windows.

"Oh dear!" he cried.

Valentina rushed toward him. "Let me help." She took one of the buckets from him, and while she tossed water out one window, the armadillo did the same out the other. Except, the river flooded in faster than they could dump it out.

"It's no use," Valentina yelled above the roar of the wind and rain. "We have to get out or we'll drown." She eyed the windows, which were too small for her and Julián to pass through.

Don Pedro gave his burrow one last glance before dropping his pail and splashing toward the main exit.

Outside, Julián used grass and mud to build a wall around the armadillo's burrow, like a fort, and when that failed, he dug the earth with his hands to form a moat. Soon that, too, became useless. Water reached past Valentina's ankles and continued creeping upward.

Doña Ruth paced. "This isn't good."

Duh, Valentina wanted to snap, but her teeth chattered. Goose bumps covered her skin. This was worse than an earthquake. A rapid, angry river would snatch you up and spit you out somewhere far away. There were hardly ever any survivors.

"We can climb up a tree!" Julián said.

Valentina glanced around her, but the trees here were thin and short, and if the flood continued, there would be little to prevent the river from swallowing them.

"These won't do," Don Pedro replied before Valentina could say anything. "We need to go deeper into the forest."

They waded away from the burrow, but Valentina could still feel the river's current pulling at her. She knew armadillos and capybaras were great swimmers and that they could hold their breath longer than humans. They might be a match for a roaring river. But Valentina and Julián didn't stand a chance. They all needed to get to safety.

The water reached halfway up Valentina's calves now, and it covered most of Doña Ruth's and Don Pedro's short legs. The capybara and armadillo swam against the current deeper into the forest, heading for higher ground. Valentina and Julián struggled to keep up, but they too managed to escape the river's grip. When they finally reached dry land, they all darted toward the thicker, taller trees.

As if sensing their retreat, rivulets of water reached toward them like tentacles feeling for prey.

"Farther!" Valentina cried.

Their feet and paws splashed on the growing puddles as the water came faster. Rain pelted them. Valentina wiped the wetness from her face, trying to keep the capybara within sight amid the darkness and storm-induced haze.

They couldn't have come this far only to be devoured by a raging river.

When it became clear they were losing the battle of outrunning the river, she yelled, "We have to climb a tree now! We don't have a choice!"

"Which one?" Julián called back.

She spotted one up ahead that would work, a thick oak that stretched toward the sky with plenty of branches to cling to. "That one!"

The river raced after them, rising even higher now, as if it had a mind of its own.

Almost. There. Only a few more feet and they'd climb to safety. But as Valentina thought this, the river rose even faster still. It came in a rush, reaching past her knees. Julián stumbled, and she held on even tighter.

Doña Ruth and Don Pedro dove beneath the water and resurfaced near the tree, but they'd barely reached the trunk when they began drifting away despite their efforts.

"The current," Don Pedro called. "It's too strong."

Doña Ruth dove in once more, but instead of getting closer, she continued moving away. She let out a few high-pitched barks.

All around them, the river swirled as if it wanted to bury them.

Fear consumed Valentina. It crept up her throat and cut off her air. She fought to remain steady, to not give in to the terror, even as the water kept creeping up. She couldn't dissolve into panic the way she'd done after the earthquake. Too many people depended on her.

They had to reach the tree—all of them. It had to be enough. *She* had to be strong enough.

She gritted her teeth, pushed against the pressure of the river keeping her from safety, and closed the last couple of feet right behind her brother—just as he stumbled and slipped beneath the water.

EIGHTEEN

"Julián!" Valentina screamed.

She felt a burst of adrenaline and, without thinking, dove toward him, grabbing his shirt before the current took him. She held him close in an almost-hug, and he clung to her, eyes wide with terror.

"Anda," she said as they reached the tree. "Go. Climb up."

The current swirled fast and strong around her now, as if it wanted to pry them away.

Julián reached toward the lowest branch and tried pulling himself up, but he barely moved a few inches before sliding back down. "I'm too tired."

"You have to try. For Mami. For Papi," she said.

"Okay." His voice was barely audible. Valentina couldn't tell if he was crying or if it was the rain on his face.

"Climb on me," she said. "It'll get you higher." She positioned herself so he could use her body as a step stool. His feet pressed into her shoulders and she winced. That would leave a bruise if they survived this. Out of the corner of her eye, she saw Doña Ruth and Don Pedro slipping farther away.

"Keep swimming," Valentina yelled at them just as Don Pedro slipped under. *He can hold his breath*, she tried to reassure herself.

"I'm trying!" The capybara's voice held a note of panic.

The pressure on Valentina's shoulders eased, and she glanced up. A momentary wave of relief surged through her as Julián settled on one of the branches, his knuckles white from gripping it tight.

He was safe—for now.

"Don't move," she told him. He didn't even try to give her one of his usual sarcastic replies. She slipped off her mochila, taking out the rope before handing him the bag. Don Pedro had resurfaced once more and was now clinging to Doña Ruth. Her thoughts stumbled over a half-hewn plan. She didn't know if it would work, but she had to try. "Do you remember the knots Papi taught us to do?"

Julián nodded.

"I need you to tie the rope around the branch. When you're done, throw it to me. I'm going after Doña Ruth and Don Pedro. Can you do that?"

Her brother nodded again and started tying the rope. Valentina fought the pull of the current with everything she had. When Julián finally threw the rope back to her, she caught it and let the current carry her back to Doña Ruth and Don Pedro. She couldn't leave them at the mercy of the river, no matter how rude the capybara had been. She just hoped the rope would be enough and that Julián's knot would stay.

"Hold on." Her muscles strained as she reached toward the capybara and armadillo with one hand, while gripping the rope with the other. She guided them in front of her.

"Oh dear," murmured Don Pedro. "That's it."

The water now reached Valentina's chest and the current threatened to pull her feet out from under her. She gripped the rope tighter. While Doña Ruth swam in front, Don Pedro clung to her with one paw and paddled with the other, and Valentina used the rope to pull them back to the tree.

Don Pedro climbed up the trunk with his claws, settling beside Julián. Doña Ruth tried to follow, but her webbed feet prevented her from getting a good grip. Eventually, between the four of them, they managed to hoist her up, and only Valentina was left in the water.

"Vale, hurry!" Julián shouted.

"I'm trying." Rain pelted Valentina, and she nearly lost her grip on the rope. *Dios mío, let me get up there.*

She thought suddenly about Albetroz. Would he be able to reach her? They were farther into the forest, and Valentina had no idea whether it was deep enough for him.

"Albetroz, I need you!"

In answer, the river pulled at her harder, as if trying to loosen her grasp.

The Dragon of the River didn't come.

Above, she heard a chorus of "you can do it," "vamos," and "try harder."

Valentina gritted her teeth. Hand over hand, she pulled herself up. Her muscles burned. Then three pairs of hands and paws were reaching down, dragging her onto the branch.

Valentina's chin wobbled, her ears whooshing with her heartbeat. She didn't trust herself to speak as she settled beside Julián. He threw his arms around her, and she let him.

She should be relieved—they were safe—but only a cold chill settled in her chest.

Around them, the storm and river roared. Their tree groaned. *Please hold. Please hold. Please hold.* She didn't know what she'd do if it didn't.

She shivered, and her face stung from the rain assaulting her. She dreamed of a hot shower, a warm bed, and her family. That was all she wanted now. Forget the art academy. Her drawings were likely ruined, anyway. Her mochila had long stopped being dry in this storm, no matter how much she tried to shield it.

From the branch opposite them, Doña Ruth called, "Thank you. For your help. You could've left us and saved yourselves, but you didn't. You came back for us."

"Of course," Valentina said. "I couldn't let you drown."

The capybara lowered her head. "I hope the queen does, indeed, help you get home to your father."

Before Valentina could reply, a creature manifested between sheets of rain. It stood several yards from them and appeared to be rising from the water. For a second, she thought, *Albetroz!* But then she saw it wasn't the diablo ballena, but rather a large human-like creature with red glowing eyes who was covered completely in hair. She knew immediately who it was: The mohán, a mischievous being who bewitched his victims, capsized boats, and guarded ancient treasure.

And made rivers flood.

"I come with a message from our queen," he boomed. "Human traitors must be disposed of. There is no room for filth in our land."

NINETEEN

The madremonte knew they were here. Of course she did. That meant someone in Tierra de los Olvidados had ratted them out. But who? Immediately she thought of Don Babou, who'd stalked out of the burrow. It had to have been him. Not even Doña Ruth had been so angry.

Valentina waited for the panic to come, but she felt only a dull emptiness.

The mohán raised his hands. Wind howled. Thunder cracked. The river rose even more, creating whirlpools that sucked in shrubs and lower branches.

Julián gripped her arm tight.

"It's okay," she told him. "We'll get out of this."

She had no idea how, though. They were trapped up a tree without a way down to safety. If only they hadn't stopped to rest. Valentina would've preferred taking her chances with the creatures of the forest to dying a watery death at the hands of the mohán.

She was terrified by the lengths the madremonte was going to in order to end them. How were they going to stay alive long enough to convince her to send them home?

A melancholic melody pulled her attention back to the creature in the river. The mohán sang a wordless song. Noise from wind and water receded to the background. Her gaze became unfocused as she stared at him. She felt the inexplicable urge to go comfort him.

No. She shook her head. She had to stay in the tree with Julián.

The mohán's song grew louder, drowning everything else out.

"Vale?"

She barely heard Julián. She leaned toward the mohán, reaching out with one hand.

"Vale!" Julián pulled her back. She felt the pressure of his fingers digging into her arm.

"I have to go," she murmured, shaking him off.

From far away, she heard Don Pedro say, "Oh dear. He's bewitching her!"

And then she didn't hear anything else. She was floating in darkness toward the hauntingly sad voice.

Slap! The stinging pain on her cheek brought her back to the present. Julián's terrified face came into focus above her as she realized she was dangling above the raging river.

She shrieked, gripping the branch tighter. She could still hear the mohán's song, but she focused on her brother. "Help me up."

With Julián's help, Valentina managed to climb back onto her branch. Once she was safe, her brother yelled at the creature, "GO AWAY!"

The mohán tilted his head, staring at them with blazing eyes.

The hair on Valentina's arms raised.

From the other side of the trunk, Doña Ruth shouted, "Summon the Dragon of the River! He is the only one capable of fighting off the mohán!"

"I tried," Valentina called back. "He didn't come."

"Try again!" Doña Ruth said. "The river has grown. He might be able to reach us now."

Valentina took a shuddering breath and nodded. Staring into the depths of the swirling river below her, which was rising higher up their tree, she said, "Albetroz! We need you! We're in trouble!"

She waited, watching as the mohán inched closer. Their tree shook as the strength of the creature's wrath intensified.

"Albetroz!" Julián yelled into the wind. "Please!"

Upstream, just barely visible in the storm, Valentina saw white foam in the churning river. The dragon broke the surface of the water and rose until he towered over the mohán. Albetroz roared—sending Valentina's teeth chattering.

He might be a comedian on a good day, but she did *not* want to get on his bad side.

The mohán screamed in fury, turning his attention away from them. Valentina hugged her brother. In the pouring rain, they watched Albetroz charge at Madremonte's messenger. They watched as the mohán dove beneath the water and as Albetroz dove after him.

Then, as suddenly as it started, the rain stopped.

Valentina blinked through the beams of sunlight washing over them, warming her skin and whisking away the wetness. As if by magic, the river receded, leaving behind a trail of sodden earth, broken branches, and stripped leaves.

Valentina loosened her stiff fingers and climbed down slowly until her boots squished on mud and she felt the steadfast ground beneath her. Julián followed behind, then Don Pedro and Doña Ruth.

It was over. They'd survived.

Valentina wished she could thank Albetroz.

"Will he be okay?" Julián asked.

"I hope so." Would Madremonte imprison him, too, for interfering with her plans and saving them?

"The Dragon of the River is a mighty force," Don Pedro said. "He will be fine."

Julián nodded, but his expression looked troubled.

"We need to get going," Valentina said. From where she stood, she could see the sun through the treetops approaching noon. Half a day gone in a poof. She didn't want to waste more time.

"Indeed," said Don Pedro, and Doña Ruth nodded.

Valentina studied them. The idea that someone had ratted them out sat like a heavy stone in her belly. Both had had a chance to send word while she and Julián slept. But the flood had threatened them, too. There was no way they would've placed themselves in danger. It *had* to have been Don Babou—right?

Julián stood at a distance, staring absentmindedly in the direction of the river. Something was wrong—she felt it in her bones—but she didn't want to ask with so many present.

"Don Pedro," Valentina said. "I'm sorry about your home. Will you be okay?"

"My dear, I will rebuild. Such is life." He smiled sadly. "It could have been much worse."

Or you could have not suffered at all. Madremonte wouldn't have sent the mohán to flood the river if Valentina and Julián had been elsewhere. The thought filled her with so much guilt she looked away. Don Pedro had lost his home because of them.

"Thank you." Valentina gave the armadillo a kiss on his scaly helmet head. "For everything. I'm—I'm sorry."

Don Pedro bowed. "My dear. It was our pleasure. I hope our queen can see how kind you are and help you go home."

Valentina sighed. "I hope so too."

She shook out her mochila, not daring to check the state of her drawings. She hoped she could salvage most of them, but right now, there was no time to lay them out to dry.

Don Pedro patted her hand, his claws remarkably gentle on her skin. "I'm quite sure you will let your heart lead you and your truth will shine through. Much luck to you in the forest. Beware the fish and other less friendly creatures in there."

Doña Ruth gave a short bark. "Yes, yes. At all costs. My heavens, do I dislike that forest." Valentina opened her mouth to say, *Well, no one's forcing you to go with us*, but the capybara hastily added, "But it is my honor to guide you. It is the least I can do for you saving our lives in the flood."

"Gracias," Valentina said, glancing over at her brother, who remained silent.

They were going through the Forest of Dreams. Despite what Doña Ruth said, how bad could it really be, especially with a guide who knew the land?

TWENTY

Valentina followed Doña Ruth through the Forest of Dreams, while her brother trailed behind them. They traveled in silence, each one seemingly lost in their own worlds, and Valentina's thoughts kept replaying the events of the last day and a half.

Finally, she couldn't take the quiet any longer. Making sure Doña Ruth was out of earshot, she turned to Julián. "What's wrong?"

He shrugged.

"We're safe now," she said. "We'll get to the madremonte, and we'll be with Papi before you know it."

"Yeah, okay." But he didn't look at her.

The knot in Valentina's belly tightened. "Julián?"

"Just leave me alone," he snapped.

Valentina frowned. She didn't want to admit it, but she needed his excitement and energy. They kept her from descending into a whirlwind of panic. She didn't know what to do with this version of Julián.

The path they followed was carved between oaks and bamboos. It was a portrait of opposites. Thick trunks and thin ones. Knotted barks and smooth ones. Leafy clusters so tight no light pierced through them, and bare branches with vines hanging from them.

Valentina cataloged the hues in her head: deep greens, bright blues, light tans. She studied the colorful birds that made the trees pop with pockets of deep purple and the fluorescent pinks and greens of lobster claw vines hanging around them. She yearned to stop and paint this landscape, but she pushed the urge away, jogging to catch up to Doña Ruth and Julián when she lagged behind.

Bumblebees buzzed between flowering bushes. A bird she'd never seen before—indigo and teal feathers with a black beak—whistled as it flew higher.

"Julián, did you see that?" Valentina asked, but her brother remained sullen.

Sunlight filtered through breaks in the leaves above them. A baby sloth the size of Valentina's hand hung on its own leafy hamaca. She reached out tentatively, and when it didn't flinch, she scratched its head. It squeaked, big round eyes looking back at her before it climbed toward others nestled in higher branches.

Valentina felt a pang as she remembered her own family, how they'd settle down in the afternoons and play board games in the living room while sipping hot chocolate and eating bocadillo slices with arequipe. She could almost taste the sweetness of the guava paste and caramel spread.

She wanted to go home.

"The forest does hold a most wondrous beauty." Valentina turned to find Doña Ruth watching her. "I have to admit, you're not exactly what I had in mind when our queen warned us about humans."

"What did she say?" Valentina asked.

"That all you do is destroy the earth and each other."

Valentina thought about her Colombia. Mami and Papi told her often about the bloody history they experienced while growing up—a war between guerrillas, paramilitaries, drug lords, and the government—that affected everyone. Car bombs happened so often when Papi was little that he said he'd always be looking over his shoulder, expecting the worst.

And one day, the worst happened in a shopping center near his house.

He was one of the lucky ones who survived.

Then there were those who were cutting down large parts of the Amazon, not caring about the animals who lived there or the damage it was doing to the earth. She thought about the images she'd seen in Mami's documentaries, of plastic in the oceans, sea turtles skewered by straws and tangled in trash.

Humans really could be awful, selfish, and greedy.

"There *are* some bad people," Valentina said finally. "But there are plenty of good ones too. My mom studies and protects the earth. Before we got here, she was studying volcanoes, trying to find out what was wrong. She's always trying to find ways to help our land and the animals in it. And Papi is the kindest person you'll ever meet." Her throat tightened, thinking of her parents. "There are many people like them."

"I see," Doña Ruth said.

The longer they hiked, the more Valentina's body ached. Her arms and legs screamed at her to rest, but she pushed herself, snacking on a few berries—which Doña Ruth had found for them—and gulping down water as she walked.

If they didn't stop, they might reach the edge of the forest by nightfall and Madremonte by morning.

At least, that's what Doña Ruth said.

Valentina still hadn't worked out what she'd say to the queen, and now with Doña Ruth here, she couldn't really talk it over with Julián. Besides, her brother seemed miles away.

She wouldn't worry about it yet. They still had some time.

After several hours, Julián stopped. "Can we take a break?"

Valentina peered up at the treetops, which enclosed them like a bubble. It was hard to see the sun from here, so she had no idea how to measure their progress. She didn't want to use Grucinda's map in front of Doña Ruth, as it might implicate the brujita further.

"Just a little bit farther," Valentina said. "We've wasted so much time."

"My dear," Doña Ruth said. "A quick rest would do us all a great deal of good. We could find more food. How is the water?"

Valentina glanced at their canteens. "I guess we could use more water, too."

But she didn't want to stop. She wanted to keep going. If they stopped, another disaster could happen. Madremonte could find and dispose of them before they even had a chance to speak with her.

Julián dropped to the ground beside a fallen tree trunk that acted as a bridge over a babbling creek. Sweat and dirt streaked his face. His brown hair stood up all over, and he had dark circles beneath his eyes.

Valentina felt a pang of guilt. He looked awful. "Okay, we'll rest, but only for a little." She turned to the capybara. "How much farther is it?"

Doña Ruth wiggled her nose. "It is still quite some ways away. Perhaps another half a day or so—all depending on the forest and if it wants to behave."

"You speak of it as if it were a person," Valentina said.

"Oh, it is, my dear. It is."

Just what they needed. She glanced around, a thump of uneasiness in her chest. What kinds of horrors could Madremonte bring through this forest?

"I shall go gather some food," Doña Ruth said. "The creek should offer clean water, but beware the fish."

Valentina nodded, taking out the canteens. This was as good a time as any to talk over their plans with her brother.

"Julián," she called. "Catch." She threw his canteen, and he caught it automatically. At least his reflexes were still intact. "Vamos, help me with this."

He scowled but walked over anyway. "What part of 'rest' don't you understand?"

"What's wrong with you? We're safe now." But for how long? Valentina uncapped her canteen and dipped it into the cool water. The gurgle of the creek rushing over sleek pebbles soothed her just as much as the water itself. She took a swig and her exhaustion lifted, replaced instead by a burst of energy. Like magic.

When Julián didn't answer, she looked up. His face was scrunched up as if he were trying not to cry.

"Hey," she said. She re-capped her canteen and put it aside. "What's up?"

He shook his head, busying himself instead with his own bottle.

"C'mon." Valentina sat beside him. "Don't you want to save Papi?"

He nodded.

"Then I need you with me. I can't do this alone."

"I hate this place," he said finally, meeting her gaze. "The madremonte. Everything. She's not supposed to hurt kids, only grown-ups, but she almost drowned us! Papi was wrong about her." He stared at his canteen. "I just want to go home and never hear about any of them ever again."

Valentina didn't know what to say—not that it mattered. Nothing she said could erase the fact that the legends he loved had become real and tried to kill them.

Impulsively, she hugged him. "It'll all work out," she murmured.

She hoped with everything she had that she was right.

TWENTY-ONE

Doña Ruth returned empty-handed. "This part of the forest is barren. Nothing but bugs."

Julián wrinkled his nose. "Gross."

That sounded more like her brother.

As they hiked, Valentina focused on coming up with a plan for convincing Madremonte. Don Pedro had told her to lead with her heart, that her truth would shine, but that was pretty much a riddle. Her heart only led home, with Mami, Papi, Julián, and her abuelitos. Besides, what *was* her truth—and what did that even mean?

The only thing she could offer the queen was the story of how they'd landed here, but how could they get Madremonte to listen before she captured—and disposed of—them? How could they guarantee that she would even *believe* their story if, by some miracle, they reached her unscathed?

Valentina sighed. The perfect solution seemed just beyond her reach. Maybe it would come to her in a burst of inspiration, like her ideas for sketches often came. She just had to be patient and open.

The deeper they went, the darker the forest became. Valentina hoped it was because the trees huddled closer together, cutting off more light, and not because the sun was setting. She didn't want to stop yet. They needed to reach the mountains.

A high-pitched giggle pulled her from her thoughts. "What's so funny?" she asked Julián.

He frowned. "I didn't laugh."

"I heard you—"

There it was again, and it definitely didn't come from her brother. Valentina peered into the dimness, trying to determine where the sound came from.

She turned to Doña Ruth. "What was that?"

"Duendes." Her whiskers twitched.

Valentina groaned. Trickster elves were naughty little beings, according to Papi. They loved getting into mischief, especially hiding people's belongings. They weren't dangerous, but they could annoy and confuse you to no end.

And Valentina didn't need any more detours.

"They're usually nocturnal creatures," Doña Ruth murmured, "which means it's likely close to nightfall now."

"What?" Valentina stopped short. "Are we close to the mountains then?"

Doña Ruth shook her head. "I'm afraid not. It seems the Bosque is playing games with us. We're barely halfway there."

"How is that possible?" From the corner of her eye, she caught Julián peering into a nearby bush, likely looking for the duendes.

Doña Ruth sighed. "The forest is fickle. It can transform itself, growing longer or shorter depending on its mood."

Valentina rubbed her temples. "We don't have time for this! At this rate, we'll never reach our father. What if we get stuck here?" The pressure in her chest grew.

Then Doña Ruth did something surprising. She ambled over and nuzzled Valentina's arm. "It will be fine, child."

The capybara's warm snout soothed her. A little.

"Can we make the forest happy? Convince it to give us back more time?" Valentina asked.

"Not likely. It responds to the earth and air around it. Lately, it seems to be in a rather foul mood. Animals have scattered from it, leaving behind only magical beings. And not the nicest of their kind, either."

The earth is not happy.

So Tierra de los Olvidados hadn't escaped damage to its land the way Valentina had first thought. What *was* the connection between her world and this one, between the earthquakes and droughts there and the foul-mood forest here? Albetroz had said the beings in this tierra were in danger of extinction, but could that be true for the forest, too? It would make sense. Animals left their habitats when it wasn't safe to live there anymore.

"Why is it in a bad mood?" Valentina asked Doña Ruth.

"Who knows, dear? Our queen has become more and more distant since she closed the borders. Perhaps the forest simply feels her despair. It seems to shift with her mood at times."

If the queen's neglect was causing harm in Tierra de los Olvidados, what did that mean for Colombia? In Papi's stories, the madremonte protected the earth, providing balance and keeping those who hurt the land in check. If she wasn't around at all in the human world anymore, perhaps that meant that the rise in natural disasters was the madremonte's fault.

Because she was absent.

Before she could ponder that idea more, Julián shouted, "I see them! There!" He bounced on his toes and pointed toward a nearby tree.

Valentina looked but didn't see anyone. "Where?"

Giggles echoed throughout the forest. A twig snapped. Valentina whirled around, only to topple over. Her shoelaces had been tied together. When she looked up from the ground, a pair of mossy-green eyes stared down at her. She screamed, scrambling to sit up.

Her outburst sent the owner of the eyes—a tiny, rosy-cheeked boy with a pointy straw hat—into a never-ending giggling fit. The entire forest shook with amusement. Even Julián and Doña Ruth chuckled.

Valentina dusted herself off and untied her shoelaces. "You know," she said, trying to keep her voice steady. "It's not polite to prank people."

"But it's so much fun," said the elf. The tip of his hat reached her knees.

"*I* didn't think so," she retorted.

"I did," Julián said. "You should've seen your face."

Valentina almost smiled as she stood. *That* was the little brother she loved and hated. In a move that reminded her too late of Mami, Valentina rested her fists on her hips. This sent everyone into a new wave of laughter. The leaves of the tall oaks shook like pom-poms.

"Glad I could be your entertainment," she said dryly.

Duendes scampered out from behind trees and bushes. About twenty elves with identical straw hats watched her. One of them, a girl with two braids, waved. Another, with black hair that spiked out beneath his hat and a guitar strapped to his back, took a bow.

The elf who'd pranked her grinned, showing off two dimples. "I'm Armando, and these are my brothers and sisters. We know Doña Ruth, but who are you?"

In spite of herself, Valentina smiled. "I'm Vale."

Her brother piped up, "I'm Julián."

"What kind of animals are you?" asked the girl with the braids.

"We're not animals," Julián said. "We're humans."

The elf's eyes widened, and Valentina groaned inwardly. She didn't want more beings knowing the truth, not when it risked their safety.

"What's *your* name?" Valentina asked her, trying to change the subject.

"Isabella." She darted behind her brothers, leaving only her braids visible.

"I won't hurt you," Valentina said.

"That's not what—" Armando started.

"Yeah, I know." Valentina sighed. "Apparently, most of you think only bad humans exist." She glanced over at Doña Ruth, who flattened her ears and gave her an apologetic look.

"So it's not true?" the duende with spiky hair asked.

Valentina shook her head. "*We're* good."

"They've been quite the lovely company," Doña Ruth added.

The elf seemed to consider that. Finally, he nodded. "I'm Carlos."

One by one, the duendes introduced themselves as they examined Valentina and Julián. They pulled their hair, sniffed behind their ears. They even opened their mouths and inspected their teeth. Valentina cringed, wanting to throw them off, but she held herself still, hoping this would convince them they meant no harm.

When they were done, Armando said, "You're like us, only bigger."

"Exactly," Valentina said. "Well, it was nice meeting you, but we must be on our way."

"No, don't go! Stay!" The chorus of chipper voices overwhelmed her.

"Can't we stay a little longer?" Julián said. "We still need to find food and water."

Valentina reached for her canteen, only to discover it was almost empty again. They'd been hiking for hours since she and Julián had refilled at the creek. She hated to admit it, but they did, in fact, need water and food. She showed Doña Ruth.

"Oh! We have both!" Isabella bounced up to them, her braids swaying as she did. "They're in our village just some ways away. Oh, please come. Please, please, please!"

"Can we?" Julián pleaded.

"Yes, do come!" The chorus of voices smacked Valentina hard. She wanted to get going, but water was crucial for survival.

She turned to Doña Ruth. "Do we have another choice?"

"It appears the duendes' offer is our best option. Nightfall is here, and we still have much ground to cover. It would be wise to rest for the night and refill our provisions, as well as map out the remainder of our route."

"I was afraid you'd say that." Valentina would have to show Doña Ruth the map to ensure they didn't go off track in the morning. She hated the idea of losing one more night.

But she didn't have a choice.

Valentina felt a knot of dread as she followed the duendes toward their village. Getting mixed up with elves was not a good idea, no matter how nice they seemed. Her brother, though, practically jumped with excitement.

Doña Ruth was the only one who shared Valentina's grim expression.

TWENTY-TWO

The village turned out to be closer than Valentina thought, and it consisted of a cluster of huts made of tree branches and clay, along with a large square at its center. A sweet, sugary scent that reminded her of cotton candy filled the air.

Surrounding the village was a narrow and quiet creek. A loose rope bridge with questionable wooden planks connected the homes with the woods. Valentina leaned over, peering into the crystalline water—and the bridge swayed, nearly tipping her over.

"Whoa." She clutched the ropes, steadying herself.

"Watch it!" Ahead of her, Julián glared before taking the last few steps and jumping onto a dusty plaza.

"Sorry," she grumbled.

"These bridges aren't meant for big people," Isabella said. The duende came up beside her, barely shifting the planks. "It helps keep Madremonte's guards away. Sometimes, anyway."

"Isabella! Shush." Armando lowered his voice, so Valentina had to lean in to hear him. "Our queen sees everyone as a threat and her guards patrol often, especially since the rumors started that someone on our land helped the men who kidnapped her son."

"Huh." That was the second time chismes were mentioned. Rumors were funny things. On the outside, they reeked of truth. But on the inside, the truth fell away like dirt in a mudslide, leaving behind a shallow shell. It was possible that someone in Tierra de los Olvidados had become a traitor. She thought briefly about the patasola blaming Grucinda for Marcos's disappearance. But it could also be Madremonte trying to blame others for her pain.

When Valentina and Isabella landed on the square, Armando pointed to the creek they'd just crossed. "You can fill your bottles there."

"I'm going to have a word with the Elders," Doña Ruth announced.

"I want to go too." Valentina didn't fully trust Doña Ruth to meet alone with the duendes, no matter how nice the capybara was acting now.

Doña Ruth shook her head. "It's best I go first. The small ones are just children. The adults . . ." She paused. "They're much less likely to be friendly with humans. They lived firsthand through La Gran Violencia."

"Did you live through it?" Valentina realized she'd never asked the capybara.

Doña Ruth shook her head. "I was born after the borders closed, and my ancestors escaped that time mostly unscathed."

Valentina nodded. She was over everyone being suspicious of them, but she could understand the capybara's point. How could she fault the duendes for believing the worst of humans if *they* had lived through humans' worst crimes? "Fine. I'll stay."

As Doña Ruth ambled deeper into the village, Julián darted away with Isabella, Armando, and Carlos.

"Sure," Valentina said sarcastically. "I'll get our water. No problem." She scowled after her brother, then sighed, kneeling on the soft, sandy dirt. Playing with the elves would distract him. He might as well enjoy the moment before they moved on.

She plunked their canteens in the creek and watched little bubbles gurgle out of the bottles. Flashes of silver swirled around her hands in the cool stream. Valentina leaned in for a better look. Tiny fish, long and sleek, seemed to be waving their fins at her.

Valentina couldn't help herself. She waved back before taking a drink.

Cool water trickled from her lips as she gulped down the entire bottle, letting it drench her parched tongue. It reminded her of sun-ripened guavas plucked from her finca. When she finished, her mouth dried. *More.* She dunked her bottle back into the creek and refilled it, then drank it in one sitting. Valentina panted as her stomach churned. Her lips puckered and the earth tilted. She took a step forward and stumbled. Her uneasiness dissolved into panic.

This wasn't right. She was feeling all wrong.

Valentina tried to stop drinking water, but the urge was too strong.

"Help." She wasn't sure if she'd said the word aloud.

"Vaaalee," her brother called. Or at least, she thought he did. He sounded so far away, as if Valentina were lying at the bottom of a river, all sounds stretched into echoes of themselves. In her fuzziness, Valentina caught Doña Ruth wobbling over, surrounded by a handful of duendes with long white beards and grumpy wrinkled faces.

"Why you look so mad?" Valentina took a few more steps and toppled over.

"What happened?" Doña Ruth asked.

"She drank water and then started acting like this," Julián said.

For some odd reason, her brother's voice made the dam inside Valentina shatter, and everything she'd held in burst out. "Papi," she wailed. "Mami." Sobbing, Valentina curled into as small a ball as she could. She was still thirsty, but the pain searing through her chest won. She was never going to see her parents again. Finding the madremonte was useless because the queen hated humans; she always would, because of what they did to her son.

The noises around Valentina were so muffled she only caught a few words: "enchanted" and "irresponsible." They sounded angry, which made her cry harder.

Valentina wept until darkness overcame her.

TWENTY-THREE

When she awoke, Valentina was in a strange place. Her head pounded, and a metallic taste lingered in her mouth. Bamboo beads covered a small window, though there was no light, just a dusty darkness. The bed on which she lay was two sizes too small, and a comforter made of real grass, vines, and periwinkle hydrangeas was draped over her.

Where was she? The last thing she remembered was kneeling by the creek, filling the bottles.

"Hello?" Her voice was hoarse. "Julián? Doña Ruth?"

The door creaked open. Valentina tensed, but the moment she saw her brother's worried face, she relaxed.

"Are you okay?" he asked.

"I think so." Drowsiness still lingered, but it had begun to lift.

Julián sat at the edge of her bed. "I was so scared. You started acting all funny and then you fainted. I thought you were dead." He hugged himself tightly, and she tried to swallow the lump that had grown too large.

"It's going to take a lot more than that for you to get rid of me," Valentina said, but she couldn't keep the tremor out of her voice. She'd been tricked so easily. She should've known better. Some truth always lingered in Papi's stories. The madremonte fiercely protected her land. The mano peluda attacked children.

Duendes couldn't be trusted at all.

She sat up fast, which sent her head into a dizzying spin.

Valentina squeezed her eyes shut until the feeling passed. "We need to get out of here. We're safer away from all of them."

"They didn't do this," Julián said. "It was the fish. They don't like strangers—it's an automatic reaction."

Even the fish had something against her. Though the words tickled something in the back of her memory, Valentina frowned. "Who told you that?"

"The Elders."

Valentina swung her legs over the bed. "I don't believe them. Where are my socks? My boots? We're going." She struggled to stand and remain upright.

Doña Ruth ambled in just then. "What are you doing? You need to rest off the magic."

"I'm not staying any longer with the duendes." Valentina tried to muster as much authority as she could. "Not when the welcome I get is being poisoned." She struggled to control her anger and fear, but they unfurled into a whirlpool—loud and fierce. All she wanted was to put as much distance as possible between them and this village, to get to the mountains and find the queen.

She was done with this journey.

"They didn't poison you," Doña Ruth said. "The fish merely enchanted you."

"*Merely?* And I don't for one second believe it was the fish. They're not the ones with the reputation of tricking people."

"Might I remind you," the capybara said softly, "your kind does not have a good reputation here either."

Her words stung. Valentina swallowed hard, the lump in her throat growing. "Then it's all the more reason to try to get rid of me, just like the madremonte wants."

Valentina couldn't help it—the tears came hot and fast again. She didn't ask to be here. She didn't ask to have a premonition about the earthquake, didn't ask for Papi to get hurt or for them to end up in this awful place.

All she wanted was to go home and pretend none of this had ever happened.

Julián slipped his arms around her, which only made her cry harder.

Doña Ruth strutted over and nudged her with her snout, which was warm and comforting. Her ears flapped, and she whistled a soothing melody. "I'm sorry some of us have misjudged you. But I know the Elders cannot lie. It's part of their code."

The fight left Valentina. It didn't matter. "We still need to get going. We need to reach the madremonte. If it means traveling through the night, then that's what we'll do."

Valentina found her backpack beside the bed and slipped it on.

"What about the creatures of the forest?" Julián asked.

"Can it be worse than what we've already come across?" Valentina said. "Like the mohán trying to drown us or the duendes' fish trying to enchant me? I don't think so."

Doña Ruth sighed. "I had a feeling you'd say that. I've filled your bottles with *good* water. I tested it myself after the Elders chased away the fish. They're not happy, by the way."

"Who? The fish?" Valentina said sarcastically. Suddenly, she remembered Don Pedro's and Doña Ruth's warnings about the fish and groaned. The capybara and Elders told the truth. *She* was the one who'd forgotten.

"The Elders feel we've placed their village at grave risk by bringing you here."

"They don't have to worry about it anymore. We're leaving." Valentina marched to the door, trying to keep her balance as best she could. Julián followed close behind.

Outside, darkness spilled onto the quiet village. In the square, five duendes greeted them with frowns. Elders, by the look of their long white beards.

One of them stepped forward. He reached Valentina's waist and had a face full of wrinkles and bushy eyebrows. He leaned on a bamboo staff.

"You must go now," he pronounced. "Far away from here. We do not meddle in the queen's business, and we shall not be held responsible for harboring the kind that hurt our land."

Valentina lifted her chin. "Don't worry. We're leaving now. We know when we're not wanted."

"Young lady." Another Elder stepped forward, this one with darker hair that curled out beneath his hat. He pointed his staff in her face. "Your lack of graciousness is further proof that our queen is just in her proclamation."

"Whatever." No matter what she said, they wouldn't believe her. She was about to say so when a loud, shrill whistle pierced through the night, making her insides turn to ice.

Everyone in the village froze.

"What was that?" Julián asked, stepping closer to Valentina.

"El silbón." Doña Ruth's eyes betrayed her fear.

According to the legend, el silbón roamed the countryside carrying a sack of bones, looking for new victims to tear to pieces. He was a death omen.

"He's been active lately, since the border alarm went off," one of the Elders murmured. "But he's far away. He won't hurt us now."

Valentina and Julián exchanged glances.

"I don't want to go if he's out there," her brother said.

Valentina put a hand on his shoulder. "We've dealt with the mano peluda and a flood. We can handle el silbón if we need to—you and me."

What Valentina didn't say was that she hoped the stories were wrong.

Another whistle pierced through the village, this one a little fainter. Valentina straightened, glancing around. The rule from the legend blazed in her brain like the neon lights at a fair: *Loud whistles mean el silbón's far away. Faint ones mean he's nearby.*

Valentina scanned the faces of the duendes. When the third whistle sounded, much softer than the first two, even the Elders looked worried. Older duendes shuffled the younger ones into their homes. A chorus of slamming doors echoed through the forest.

"Doña Ruth, how fast can you run?" Valentina asked.

"Fast enough to get out of here and away from el silbón," she said proudly. "The question is, how fast can a human girl run?"

Valentina didn't get to answer. Another whistle sounded, this one a faint murmur, and the hairs on the back of her neck stood. This was not good.

Just then, a duende cried, "Felipe! Where are you, Felipe?"

Valentina spun around.

An elf stood in the middle of the village plaza, her hands clenched in the fabric of her skirt. Her hat sat askew, and tears streamed down her face.

"Felipe," the woman wailed.

Valentina tensed. The duende's desperation took her breath away.

Doña Ruth nudged her. Julián tugged her arm. She looked away from the duende woman, and that was when she saw el silbón—a tall, bony man with an oversized hat and a sack hung over his shoulders. He loomed over a tiny, shivering elf, his skeletal face breaking into a terrifying grin.

TWENTY-FOUR

Valentina whirled to face Doña Ruth and Julián. Her brother stared at her, wide-eyed, and she could feel the terror rolling off him. The capybara stood frozen.

Nope. This wasn't good.

A whimper pulled her attention back to the baby elf. "Mamá," he cried.

Duendes hid in their huts, peeking out of round windows. Only Felipe's mother stood in the plaza, still as stone. She didn't run to her son, but she didn't flee, either.

El silbón leered at Felipe, showing a mouthful of sharp yellow teeth.

"I heard there's some troublemakers hiding here," he said tauntingly. His voice was as thin and rough as his bony body. "You one of 'em?" He shook his bag, which rattled—*like bones*.

Felipe shrank back.

Anger shot through Valentina. Felipe was just a kid, much younger than Julián. Why did bullies always think they could pick on those who were smaller than them? Her hands curled into fists.

"Vale." Her brother gripped her arm. "Let's go. While he's not looking."

They *could* go now. El silbón was distracted. They could be out of the village and in the cover of the forest before he realized it. But what would happen to Felipe? To his mother? To the other duendes?

El silbón had come for her and Julián—the "troublemakers." Had the madremonte sent him? It didn't matter. Felipe's life was in danger because of them. If they left, they were as bad as the queen made them out to be. They would be no better than the men who kidnapped her son. Papi would never forgive them. He'd always told her, "We have a responsibility to help those around us."

Valentina knew what she had to do, though the thought of it made her sick. Before she could change her mind, she whispered to Doña Ruth, "Go with Julián. Hide. I'll be right back."

"Vale." Julián's eyes flashed with fear. "What are you doing?"

Valentina couldn't meet his gaze. She thought of all the things that could go wrong. El silbón could catch her and dump her bones in his bag. She could be separated from Julián, maybe forever, and never see her family again.

Was she really going to do this?

"That guy needs to pick on someone his own size." There was more conviction in her words than she felt. "I'll be fine. Just stay out of his way."

"Are you sure, dear?" Doña Ruth asked.

"Yes," Valentina hissed. "Go!"

Doña Ruth and her brother slipped away, blending into the trees. That was one good thing about nighttime—you could hide from monsters.

She turned back to el silbón. Now he gripped Felipe by the shirt, the little duende's feet wiggling a few feet off the ground.

"Hey!" she yelled without thinking.

El silbón twisted his head toward Valentina—almost 180 degrees. Cold sweat swept over her. A sliver of moonlight hit el silbón square in the face, and Valentina could see what she'd missed before. Where his eyes should have been, dark, gaping holes stared back at her.

Her legs threatened to give out.

She sucked in a breath, steadying herself, then grabbed a handful of dirt and pebbles and threw them at el silbón. She spit out with as much venom as she could, "Leave. Him. Alone."

El silbón's body followed his head, his attention now completely on Valentina. He dropped Felipe, and the little duende darted to his mother. The two scurried into one of the nearby huts, slamming the door behind them.

Now that she could see el silbón fully, Valentina saw that he did, in fact, have skin. It simply stretched tight over the bones like overworked leather.

"Little girl," he rasped. "So far away from your home. My lucky day to find you so quickly."

He sauntered toward Valentina.

She held his gaze, her heartbeat whooshing in her ears. Her skin prickled, but she forced herself to stand still, a half-hatched plan beginning to form. *Just a little closer* . . . When he was merely yards away, Valentina bolted.

Away from Doña Ruth and Julián.

Away from the village, over the rickety bridge.

Away from the duendes and the fish and the enchantments.

All she could think of was getting el silbón as far away from the village as possible.

Her feet pounded the hard earth. Her backpack bounced against her. She gulped down air as she pushed her aching legs farther. She didn't stop to think about how she'd get back. Behind her, el silbón's whistling was a faint whisper.

He was too close.

Which meant he was still a threat to her, to her brother, to the village.

TWENTY-FIVE

Valentina ran over rocks and streams, under vines and branches, el silbón's whistles steady behind her. When she tripped and fell, she jumped back up and pushed herself even more, darting left, then right. She zigzagged and circled around in the Bosque de Sueños, hoping to confuse el silbón.

Hoping he'd get dizzy and give up.

Another whistle pierced the darkness, louder this time. *It's working!* He was getting farther away. A surge of energy shot through her and she sprinted deeper into the woods. As she did, she turned the legends over in her head, trying to find something she could use against him in case her plan failed.

What was el silbón afraid of? Whips. Red pepper. Dogs. She didn't have the last two, but maybe she could make a whip.

Valentina stopped running then. She gasped for air as she searched for anything that could work. Branches. Leaves. Vines. The whistles kept coming, but they were louder. Farther. As if he was moving away from her. *Good,* she thought. *Go back to your queen.*

Still, she wasn't letting her guard down. As quickly as she could make her trembling fingers work, she snapped some low-lying branches from nearby trees. "I'm sorry," she murmured. "I need this to keep us safe. Thank you for your gift."

She felt weird speaking to trees, but everything she'd learned about the forest—how it was a living, temperamental thing—told her this was the right thing to do. She found some vines and wild grass, which she tied to the edges of the branches, leaving her with two makeshift whips.

Not her best work, but it would have to do.

Valentina strained to hear el silbón's whistles. But the forest had turned quiet, save for the cicadas chirping relentlessly. A horrifying thought suddenly occurred to her: The queen's guard wouldn't go back empty-handed, would he? Did she just leave her brother and the others completely exposed?

Fear thrummed in her chest.

"No, no, no," she groaned. She had to find her way back to the duendes and her brother and Doña Ruth.

Armed with the two improvised whips, Valentina started back toward the village. She realized with growing dread, though, that she had no idea how to get back. Not only was the forest engulfed in shadows, but she'd lost her way with all the turns she'd taken.

How was she supposed to get back to her brother now?

Valentina's head jerked in every direction, scanning her surroundings. Every tree looked the same. Each bush identical. A thrum of panic suffocated her.

It's okay, she told herself. *You're okay. You can do it.*

It didn't help. She was lost, and her brother was out there somewhere in these terrible woods, and so was el silbón. She would make it this far only to be bested by this land, and she'd never save Papi, never get back home.

Valentina squeezed her eyes shut, struggling to keep her panic from overflowing.

Then she remembered the map tucked away in her mochila.

Letting out a breath, she sifted through her bag until she found the parchment. With the flashlight, she located her *V* and, a few inches away, in a circle labeled CIUDADELA DE DUENDES, she saw Julián's *J*. Relief washed over her. He was safe. She took a few steps in each direction until she knew exactly which way the village lay.

Then a shrill whistle pierced through the forest. In the direction of the village.

Julián! Valentina stashed the map, gripped a branch in each hand, and darted back to the duendes. *Faster,* she urged herself. But she was so tired. Her muscles screamed. As she got closer, the air turned musky, sweet. She was almost there.

The old wooden bridge was in sight when she heard it—a terrified shriek she'd know anywhere, followed by a series of short barks.

"Julián!" Valentina screamed. "Doña Ruth!"

The only response was a steady, faint whistling. El silbón was close by.

Her brother screamed again. Then absolute silence.

"I'm coming, Julián!" Valentina bellowed, her chest heaving. She couldn't lose her brother. She dashed across the bridge aglow in torchlight and skidded to a stop in the open square.

"Julián!" Valentina yelled again. "Doña Ruth!"

Neither answered her.

Duendes streamed out of their homes, but her brother and the capybara were nowhere in sight. She stared desperately at the elves. Their mouths moved, but she couldn't hear them.

"Where are they?" she demanded.

One of the Elders approached her. "El silbón is gone."

Valentina pressed her knuckles against her thighs and folded over, struggling to catch her breath. She didn't care about that monster. "My brother. Doña Ruth. Where. Are. They?"

The Elder bowed his head. "We don't know. Your quick thinking allowed us time to fetch the dogs, but then we heard the scream. I am afraid we might have been too late."

"No!" Valentina snapped. "It's not too late. Help me find them!" Her voice hitched. They had to be okay. Maybe el silbón almost got them, but they tricked him like she had tricked him.

"Search the forest," another Elder ordered. Duendes young and old flooded the surrounding area, searching in bushes, through foliage. They held torches ablaze with fire, casting long golden shadows everywhere.

Valentina followed them, looking up trees and calling out for her brother and Doña Ruth. *Please be okay,* she pleaded silently over and over. *I promise I'll never get mad at you again. Just be okay.*

Valentina and the duendes searched everywhere, but Julián and Doña Ruth had disappeared.

After a while, Valentina found the spot where they must've hidden. The grass had been flattened against the dirt and branches from the nearby berry bush were torn. Valentina peered into the deep foliage around her and noticed a trail of discarded berries and broken branches, as well as a single set of footprints: the capybara's.

"Julián!" Valentina called.

No response. Where were Julián's footprints? Maybe he'd ridden on Doña Ruth's back. Or maybe the capybara had abandoned him.

No, she wouldn't have done that. "Doña Ruth!"

Valentina followed the trail, gripping the torch so tight her hands hurt. But a few feet ahead, everything stood intact. The trail had vanished. Valentina turned, looking back at the patches of grass, the bushes of berries, the trunks of oaks surrounding her. Nada. No sign of them.

It was like they'd simply evaporated . . . or like someone had picked up them up.

Someone like el silbón.

Valentina shook those thoughts out of her head. She waved the torch around, trying to find their trail again. When it became clear there was nothing on the ground, she turned her attention upward.

A bright flicker caught Valentina's eye. Frowning, she peered into the trees until she found the source. Hanging from a small branch was a thin, gold chain with a crucifix—just like the one Mami had given Julián for his fifth birthday.

TWENTY-SIX

"Julián!" Valentina shrieked. This couldn't be happening. Not now, after everything they'd been through. Her hands shook as she slipped the chain off the branch. "Vamos," she pleaded into the night. "Come out. El silbón's gone. It's safe now."

Nothing but silence and the cicadas' chirps answered her.

Even the wind seemed to have paused.

She stared vacantly into the shadows, hoping that at any moment Julián would poke his head out from the bushes, roll his eyes at her, and tell her she was no fun. That she worried too much. Her vision blurred. This was worse than seeing Papi fall. At least then she'd still had her brother.

Now she was alone.

Valentina's legs gave out, and she dropped to the ground, burying her face in her hands. The cool metal of the crucifix bit into her cheek. She didn't even know where to look for him and Doña Ruth. She had the map in her mochila, but the idea of heading out into the Bosque de Sueños by herself terrified her—though the thought of what el silbón might do to her brother and Doña Ruth scared her even more.

Beside her, someone cleared their throat. She lifted her head to find the Elder with the wrinkled face and bushy eyebrows studying her. "They're not here."

Valentina heard him as if she were submerged underwater.

She knew he was right, of course. Her heart refused to believe el silbón had taken Julián and Doña Ruth, but that was the only thing that made sense. What would happen to them now? Doña Ruth would likely be taken captive, not killed, but what about Julián? Would el silbón dispose of him—Madremonte's orders and all that? After all, the patasola had been ready to execute them on the spot. Would el silbón be the same?

"Let us go back to the village," the Elder was saying.

Valentina's attention shifted to the duende. "Why? You said we put your village at risk. And we did. El silbón came and almost hurt Felipe. He took my brother."

The Elder's expression softened. "You risked your safety to protect one of our people. It is the least we can do."

She took a deep breath and stood, her fingers curling around the crucifix. "I have to find them. I have to go after el silbón." She had to get her brother back before it was too late.

The Elder's gaze darted around. "It is best to continue this conversation in the safety of the village."

It dawned on her how nervous he was, and how exposed they all were here in the open. It was clear the queen's guards had been one step ahead. Madremonte probably had spies everywhere! But it seemed like the Elder wanted to help. Maybe Valentina wouldn't have to find Julián alone. She slipped her brother's chain around her neck and tucked it under her shirt, next to her locket. Then she nodded and followed the duendes back to the village.

When they reached the open square, the Elder ordered everyone to their huts except for a group of older elves. "We shall convene an assembly," he said, his voice grave. "The human girl will come with us."

"Valentina."

The Elder peered at her from beneath his bushy eyebrows. "Excuse me?"

"Um, my name." Her fingers fidgeted with the strap of her mochila. "It's Valentina."

"Forgive me." The Elder dipped his head. "Valentina will join us."

She followed them into one of the huts and squeezed into a chair a few sizes too small. Everyone spoke in hushed voices, and she didn't miss the furtive glances they sent her way. Her knees jiggled while they waited. She didn't want to sit still. She wanted to be out there, finding Julián. But she needed whatever help the duendes would give her.

Finally, the Elder with the bushy eyebrows—the leader, Valentina guessed—banged his gavel. The murmur in the room instantly hushed.

"My fellow compadres," he said, meeting every duende's gaze. "It is clear we have misjudged the human girl. Valentina risked her life to save one of ours, and we are in her debt."

A murmur trickled through the group of duendes. Most of them nodded, though a few frowned at her, especially an Elder with dark, graying hair who looked younger than the rest. He sat with his arms crossed, a scowl on his face.

"Our code dictates," the head Elder continued, "that if aid is rendered, then aid must be repaid. Young Valentina has lost one of her own, so I propose we help her find him."

Valentina leaned forward, relief washing over her. She wouldn't have to do this alone. They were really going to help.

"Objection," the dark-haired Elder called out. "It is simply not safe. We will be marked."

She fought a groan. It wouldn't be that simple. Why would it? Nothing had been simple since getting to this cursed land.

"Perhaps," the head Elder countered. "But have we not already been subjected to a search when the queen sent el silbón here? She has suspected our village since the days of young Marcos's disappearance, even though our kind suffered at the hands of humans as well. We had no reason to engage in that sort of treason. And yet here we are. Our queen's guard crossed the line when he threatened our most innocent."

Valentina hung her head as the others glanced at her. Would they ever see her as anything other than the worst of her kind?

Then she processed what the head Elder had said. El silbón was the queen's guard. She'd been right. The madremonte had sent el silbón after them. It *was* their fault Felipe was threatened.

"Perhaps," the dark-haired Elder said. "But you are suggesting helping our enemy. Did you forget how they destroyed our village? How they took our young?"

That wasn't us, Valentina fumed.

"I could never forget, José," the head Elder said quietly. "My wife and children disappeared because of humans."

Valentina stared at him, horrified. "I'm so sorry," she whispered. She met his gaze, and in his eyes, she saw only sadness.

José shook his head. "How did they even get here? The border has been shut for over three hundred years. How do a pair of human children suddenly appear in Tierra de los Olvidados?"

Valentina wished she understood that herself. But maybe if she told the duendes everything that had happened, they would help her, just as Don Pedro and Doña Ruth had back by the river. Tentatively, she raised her hand.

When the head Elder nodded toward her, Valentina said, "Everything I've heard about my people since coming to Tierra de los Olvidados has been horrible, and I don't blame you for not trusting us. *I* wouldn't trust us, either. Just because a lot of time passes doesn't mean that the hurt others have done to you goes away. That's what my papi says when he talks about the family he lost."

She paused, fiddling with Julián's crucifix, and then she told them about the earthquake and Papi, about the tunnel and Grucinda's cottage, about Albetroz and the mohán, and everything else that had brought them to this village and this moment.

"I don't know how we passed through the border," she finished, "but I need to find the madremonte and my brother. We need to go back home and save my father." She glanced around the room, expecting to find faces full of disbelief. Instead, she saw most of the Elders were nodding.

"The human speaks truth," one of them said.

Don Pedro had said something similar. Then her thoughts buzzed with excitement: Could convincing the madremonte be that easy—just tell the truth?

"But how did she get through the border?" another asked. "Could the enchantments be failing?"

"Perhaps some force is working against the queen," suggested a third.

José scowled. "It is a mistake to confide in a human."

The head Elder replied, "The fact remains, she is here and she needs our help—though first, we need to determine where her brother and Doña Ruth were taken."

"Grucinda gave us a map," Valentina said slowly. Why hadn't she thought about it earlier? "It shows our location. Maybe it'll show where my brother is."

She took the parchment out of her mochila, hoping it would still work with her and Julián separated. She studied the squiggles and lines and found her *V* in the village. Her gaze drifted toward the top right and the Cordillera Monumental, where the queen lived.

And there, right inside the sketch that read MADREMONTE'S CASTLE, was a glowing *J*.

"She has him," she whispered. "He's still alive."

At least, Valentina hoped that was how the map worked. As long as he was alive, his *J* would show. Doña Ruth didn't have her own letter on the parchment, and Valentina hoped with all her heart the capybara was also alive and with Julián.

"It is settled," the head Elder said. "Valentina needs to reach the queen's castle, and we will help her get there." He turned to her. "We can't promise Madremonte will hear you. But we can promise to help you reach her."

"Gracias." Valentina swallowed her fear. "When can we go?"

"Now, if you wish."

"Yes." It wasn't that Valentina wanted to trek through the dark forest, but she refused to waste any more time. And every stop gave the queen a chance to send more guards after her.

"Very well. I shall call your guides and prepare some provisions. They will take you to the edge of the forest, which lies at the foot of the mountains. From there, Condor will fly you to the castle. We shall arrange it."

"You won't go with me all the way?" Valentina asked, not sure she wanted to put her trust in a flying bird she hadn't met yet.

The Elder shook his head. "It is much too dangerous for us outside the forest." He banged his gavel and everyone dispersed.

Valentina left the hut and waited in the empty plaza, watching the torchlights on the huts flicker. Sweat soaked her shirt and clung to her skin. Anxiety hummed through her body. She walked over to the creek and filled her water bottle—after making sure there weren't any fish, of course. She'd learned her lesson.

"Are you ready?"

The familiar voice startled her. Valentina whirled around and found Armando and Isabella watching her.

"Yes," she said.

"Good," Armando said. He handed her a sack full of fruits and nuts.

Valentina peered inside and groaned inwardly. Moras and guayabas. As much as she loved blackberries and guavas, she was starting to tire of all the fruits. She'd give anything for some arepas with fresh scrambled eggs and some steaming hot chocolate. Still, she wouldn't be ungrateful.

"Thanks," she said, placing the fruits in her bag. "You're part of my group?"

"We are your guides." Armando bowed. "At your disposal, señorita."

"But—" She looked between him and Isabella. "You're just kids."

"So are you," Isabella pointed out.

"I have no choice," Valentina said. "My brother and father need me."

"And we love adventure," Armando said simply, his eyes twinkling.

It could be way worse. She could be stuck with José, who would probably try to push her off the edge of a cliff. Not that she would blame him.

Valentina smiled at Armando and Isabella. "Deal."

The entire village emptied onto the square to see them off. Many duendes waved. Some even clapped when they saw Valentina. The little one—Felipe—threw himself at her ankles.

"Show that mean silbón who's boss," he whispered, then darted back to his mami, who mouthed, *Gracias*.

And Valentina would show el silbón a thing or two when they met again. Because she would stop at nothing to get her brother back.

TWENTY-SEVEN

The forest on this side of the village was dense. In her panic earlier, Valentina had barely noticed, but now she couldn't miss the overgrown bushes or the thick tapestry of leaves above her. Only a few slivers of moonlight pierced through, giving the forest a silvery halo.

But for once, she didn't feel like painting the scene.

All she could think about was her brother. She imagined him shivering in some dungeon, alone and afraid. And that was the best-case scenario. It was her fault he got captured. If they'd run like he'd asked, if she hadn't tried to lure el silbón away on her own, then they might still be together.

But Felipe . . .

Valentina sighed, tightening the straps on her mochila. She knew she'd done the right thing for the little duende, but she couldn't shake off the guilt. Her decision had put her brother in danger. If something happened to him, her parents would never forgive her. *She* would never forgive herself.

No, she wouldn't let herself go there.

As they trekked through the dark forest, her belly churned with uneasiness. She appreciated the duendes' help, she really did, and she was glad not to be alone, but how much help could a pair of kid elves be against the madremonte's guards? They barely reached her knees and had no magic. Not even Grucinda had been able to fight off the patasola.

"You okay up there?" Isabella asked. "You're awfully quiet."

"I'm fine," Valentina said. They wouldn't understand.

They traveled through the night. With every hoot and howl, Valentina jumped, waiting for another monster to come out of the shadows, but except for the nuisance of some giant mosquitoes, the journey was mostly unremarkable.

When early-morning rays broke through the foliage, Valentina paused and took out the map. Her *V* blinked up at her, closer now to the edge of the forest. And her brother's *J* glowed inside the castle.

"How much longer?" she asked Isabella and Armando as they kept going, trudging through overgrown shrubs.

"Well, it gets denser before it starts thinning out again," Isabella said.

"And we haven't passed Jaguar's home," Armando added. "Right after that it's a short walk. Condor will meet us near the third peak past el Cañón de la Muerte."

Death's Canyon sounded like a place she should avoid at all costs.

Valentina sighed. Why was it no one in this world could give her a straight answer? Like, *You're three hours away at this pace.* Or, *In another eight miles we'll be at the mountains.* She could feel her frustration spiraling, and she didn't want to admit that the sameness and denseness of the forest were suffocating her. The map was the only way she knew they were on track, inching closer to the Cordillera Monumental. The texture of the parchment and the glow of Julián's *J* made her feel more grounded.

As they continued through the morning, Valentina started wondering if the Bosque de Sueños was playing tricks on them again. They should've been there by now, right? She checked the map again, and sure enough, they'd only moved a little to the northeast.

What would it take to get the fickle forest on her side for once?

It didn't help that Isabella and Armando seemed to think this was some fun expedition. They spent a good part of their journey narrating each plant and animal they encountered.

"Those are labios de mujer," Isabella said in one spot, gesturing to a cluster of plants with crimson flowers and green leaves that reminded Valentina of red puckered lips.

"Pretty," Valentina said through gritted teeth. The plant answered her with a melodic, tinkling "Gracias," and the sound sent a burst of iridescent blue-and-black butterflies fluttering around them.

What Valentina had *really* wanted to say, though, was: *¡Vamos! This is a rescue mission. There's no time for sightseeing!* Perhaps at another time, when everything she loved wasn't at risk of being snatched away, she would have actually enjoyed the tour. Even now, a small part of her just wanted to sit in wonder and draw everything.

But she couldn't. Not when so much was at stake.

When they tired of being guides, the duendes took to playing tag, darting between bushes and behind trees, sometimes running ahead so much, Valentina lost sight of them before they returned, laughing. They tried to engage her, but she simply marched ahead, growing more frustrated as the morning stretched on.

Finally, Valentina had enough. "I wish you'd stop messing around!" she said, her face flushed with anger. "My brother's been captured and who knows what Madremonte will do to him, and all you can do is play?"

"Sorry," Isabella mumbled, tugging on her braids.

"We're just trying to make the time go faster," Armando said sheepishly.

Valentina stomped away, and the duendes scrambled after her, pulling her in the right direction. They set off at an even pace, and Valentina was relieved when they remained focused. She felt a little bad for yelling at them. They couldn't understand how serious this was. It wasn't their brother who'd been taken.

After a while, Isabella said softly, "Our queen won't hurt him, you know."

Armando ducked under low branches and shifted left. Here, the earth sloped slightly upward. "She'll probably wait until she has you. He's kind of like bait."

Valentina felt sick. She would have to find Julián before Madremonte found her.

Papi always said, "Between being kind and being right, choose kind." But how could she be kind to a queen who'd tried to drown them? Who'd kidnapped her brother? Who wanted them dead?

Soon, the trees grew taller and closer together, the treetops bunching up and covering more sunlight. Here, the vegetation was a mix of palm trees and oaks, dotted with ferns. Small brown birds with orange-and-black crests on their heads, like crowns, sat atop the branches. One of them cocked its head and studied them.

"Those are royals," Isabella said. "They're only found here, in the thickest part of the forest, so that means we'll be at the mountains before you know it."

Valentina felt a slow lifting of the invisible weight she'd been carrying. They were almost there. Condor would be waiting for her, and she would find her brother. Together, they would convince Madremonte to help them.

They would go home.

Not that Isabella and Armando felt her urgency. They had slipped back into their playfulness. They jogged in place at first, then started darting behind trees and hiding from each other. Valentina groaned as they ran ahead.

"Hey!" she cried. "Stop doing that!"

But all she heard was the tinkling of laughter and a "Don't worry so much!" as the two duendes disappeared in the foliage. They were officially worse than her brother.

Valentina gripped the straps of her mochila and marched on in the direction the duendes had gone, furious. She wouldn't slow down just because they wanted to have fun. Let *them* find *her* once they were done playing.

After a while, though, Valentina realized she couldn't hear the duendes anymore. Fear knotted in her belly. "Isabella?" she called out. "Armando?"

A howler monkey returned her call, but no duendes appeared.

How long had it been since she last saw them? She took out the map and studied it—and almost fell to her knees. Instead of going northeast toward the mountains, the way they'd been traveling, she'd gone *south*east. She was still heading toward the Cordillera Monumental, but now she was even farther from the meeting point with Condor.

And worse yet, she was completely alone.

TWENTY-EIGHT

No, no, no!

How could this have happened? Had the duendes ditched her? That didn't make sense. They could've just kicked her out of the village and let her fend for herself. Besides, they'd proven themselves, even when she'd still had some reservations.

She must've gone too fast in the wrong direction, or the forest had tricked her—again.

Either way, now she was lost and she'd have to find her brother on her own. The familiar panic thrummed in her chest, but she forced herself to push it down. She couldn't fall apart. Not with Julián and Papi counting on her.

At least she had the map. She studied it again. Directly to the east, between the mountains and forest, was a river—Río de Lágrimas. Maybe she didn't have to keep traveling through this moody forest. Papi always said that if you got lost in the wilderness, you should find water, because it would lead you to safety. She hoped that was true here in Tierra de los Olvidados, too. And she liked the idea of hiking near the mountains much more than continuing through the forest, even if the memory of the madremonte's flood still haunted her.

Valentina just hoped Condor would wait for her at el Cañón de la Muerte.

Without Armando and Isabella, Valentina kept a swifter pace. The longer she hiked, the more she noticed a change in flora. Palms with scratches on their trunks towered over ceibas and other trees she didn't recognize. The mixture of plant life was eclectic, as if the earth couldn't decide which species to breed, so it had them all. Then palm trees began to overrun the others, and the mix of jungle and palms reminded her of the Cocora Valley in the Andes. It made her feel light-years away from her world and her family.

Sweat trickled down Valentina's face. Her T-shirt clung to her skin. Every time she inhaled, humid heat suffocated her. But she knew she was getting closer to the Río de Lágrimas and the mountains, thanks to the map, and it seemed the forest was finally playing nice.

Too little, too late, Valentina thought crossly.

She knew Julián was still in Madremonte's castle. Every time she checked to make sure she was on track, she also checked on Julián. And every time, his *J* blinked angrily at her, as if saying, *C'mon, Vale, what's taking you so long?*

"I'm coming," she said at one point, startling a few birds, who squawked and flew away. She shook her head. "I'm officially losing it."

How much time had passed? Judging by the light filtering through the treetops, it was still day—a small relief.

Valentina had to keep going, but her stomach grumbled. She stashed the map and paused a moment to snack on the nuts and fruits the duendes had given her. She missed Armando and Isabella. Were they looking for her? Or had they returned to the village?

She'd barely scooped out a handful of nuts when a howler monkey swung overhead and swiped the sack from her fist.

"Hey!" she yelled, running after it.

But the monkey simply howled and howled, climbing higher away from her.

"Are you kidding me?!" Even the wildlife had something against her.

A soft, lazy voice said nearby, "Why are you yelling so much?"

Valentina gripped the strap of her bag, peering into the foliage. She circled around until her gaze settled on a brown-gray lump hanging upside down from the branch of a nearby tree. When two sleepy black eyes stared back at her, Valentina gasped. "Oh!"

A sloth stretched on the branch, barely raising his head. He yawned. Then, in slow motion, he reached for the trunk, righting himself. "Do you always look so scared?"

Valentina glared at him. "I don't look scared."

The sloth, however, grinned. His eyes blended with the black fur around them, which made him look like he was wearing a mask. A smile tugged at her own lips.

"I'm not scared," Valentina repeated, her voice softer. "I'm frustrated. Those monkeys just took my food."

"Oh, now, that wasn't nice." The sloth studied her, every movement unhurried and relaxed. "You're a long way from home, no?"

"It's a long and complicated story." Valentina sat on the buttress root of the tree. "Would you happen to know how far the river is from here? The map says I'm close, but I can't seem to get there."

"Why, yes. It's just on the other side of this cluster of trees." The sloth pointed to Valentina's right. "About a mile that way."

"Yes!" she said, pumping a fist into the air. Finally, someone with a straight answer.

Her feet ached and she was exhausted, but for the first time since her brother was taken, a burst of hope filled her. At the river, she could fill her canteens, and if Condor waited for her, maybe she could even reach Julián—and Madremonte—by nightfall.

"Would you be a dear and bring me some of the leaves from that tree behind you?" the sloth said.

"Of course." Valentina snapped a few round ones and brought them over to the sloth.

"Mil gracias." He gave her a sleepy smile as he chewed.

"You're not afraid of me."

"Why would I be?"

"Because everyone on this land seems to be." Even as she said it, she knew it wasn't quite true. Grucinda, Albetroz, and Don Pedro hadn't been afraid. Doña Ruth's initial hostility had faded after the flood. And while some of the duendes feared her, others, like Armando and Isabella, hadn't.

Valentina had also been unfair to the duendes. She'd mistrusted them because of stories she'd heard. Rumors. How could she get mad at them when she had done something similar?

"Ah." The sloth chewed, his eyes closed. "Madremonte has become lost in her pain. She forgets we knew kind humans once too. But I, for one, do not. If it weren't for a human, my great-grandfather would have died."

"Really?"

"Indeed. My ancestor found himself caught in a trap in your world, and a farmer saved him. Set him on his way." The sloth smiled, lost in some memory. "We had a prosperous partnership then. Peace existed between both lands. There was no need for borders. Ah, those were the golden years." He sighed. "Times change, of course. But an intelligent mind, no matter how slow, knows that living creatures can be neither all good nor all evil. Our queen seems to have forgotten that in her grief."

The sloth dropped his legs and grasped the tree trunk with his claws. "Would you care for company to the river? It's been so long since I've been there. The trees near the riverbank have the tastiest leaves." He grinned. "More sunlight."

"Ay sí!" She didn't like being alone with her thoughts in this jungle, and she had taken to the sloth. He reminded her of a quieter Don Pedro. "I'm Valentina, by the way."

"So very pleased to meet you. I'm Don Perezoso. I'm afraid I'm not too quick, however. Would you mind carrying me?"

Valentina smiled. "Not at all." She reached out, and the sloth curled against her, all warm and fuzzy, like Julián used to do when he was a baby. Her throat tightened at the memory.

With Don Perezoso directing her, Valentina pushed quickly through the rest of the jungle. They hadn't walked too long when they came across a large ceiba, whose buttress roots towered over Valentina. She couldn't climb them, and they extended in all directions like an endless barrier.

"We need to cross over," Don Perezoso said. "There."

Valentina saw it: an opening in the thick trunk of the ceiba, three times as wide as her and twice as tall. "We have to go through that?"

"Yes. I don't remember this path being so blocked."

"How long has it been since you came this way?"

"Too long."

Valentina tried not to let his words worry her. Don Perezoso might be nice and much-needed company, but what if he wasn't the most reliable guide? What if he misremembered?

I have the map, she reminded herself. That would keep her from getting lost.

Don Perezoso hung on loosely as Valentina took a step into the dark opening of the ceiba. She paused, letting her eyes adjust. Moss clung to the walls of the small cavern, and it smelled like old, damp wood. In the distance, Valentina caught a halo of light.

The exit.

She pressed against the inner wall of the ceiba, afraid to walk through the middle. She couldn't stop imagining herself floating down into an abyss, like Alicia in el País de las Maravillas. But she wasn't Alice, and this wasn't Wonderland. Who knew what horrors might lurk within this tree?

"That's it," the sloth said softly. "You've got it."

Valentina measured each step. Not too quickly, not too slowly. She had only one good hand to hold on with—the other gripped Don Perezoso—and nothing to hold on *to.*

When they finally reached the other side, Valentina and the sloth broke into yet another part of the forest. Lower palms opened wide in the mist. Ferns dotted the ground, along with bushes bursting with fruit she didn't recognize. But best of all, there, beyond the last mammoth ceiba, was the bank of a river. Sunlight spilled over it, and nothing had ever looked so beautiful.

"We're here!" she cried. "Thank you!"

"You're most welcome." Don Perezoso yawned and stretched, then pointed ahead. "If you don't mind, that tree over there looks quite inviting."

Gently, Valentina rested him on the lowest branch. "Chao, Don Perezoso. Thank you."

"Adiós, kind Vale."

Kind. She hoped Madremonte and her spies could see this, and that by the time Valentina reached her, the queen would be willing to help them without resistance.

She wouldn't hold her breath.

The sound of rushing water pulled her forward until she reached the riverbank, where the current before her swished furiously. It moved fast, water crashing over rocks, reminding her of the treacherous Cauca River back home. A quick glance at the map confirmed she was, indeed, at the Río de Lágrimas and that Julián was still in Madremonte's castle.

Falling to her knees, she peered into the water, looking for flashy silver fish. When she was certain nothing would try to enchant her, she cupped her hands and splashed her face. Ice-cold water dripped down her face and neck, instantly cooling her. She refilled her canteens and took a sip, feeling the now familiar burst of energy course through her.

Then Valentina forced herself to stand. She glanced up, studying her surroundings.

On the other side of the river, reaching toward the cloudless sky, were the snow-covered peaks of the Cordillera Monumental.

TWENTY-NINE

Valentina studied the map to ground herself. She found el Cañón de la Muerte, her meeting point with Condor, north of where her *V* blinked and close to Madremonte's castle.

All she had to do was follow the river toward the canyon, where hopefully Condor would still be waiting—without running into any of the queen's guard.

With a final glance at the trees where she'd left Don Perezoso, she began walking along the riverbank toward the north. A few rose-gold fish splashed against the current. They seemed to be going upstream, like her. Palms swayed in the breeze. The canopies that had kept the sun from her inside the forest now teemed with caws and howls and an incessant buzz of insects. Just then, a group of macaws flew from the treetops in bursts of reds, yellows, blues, and greens.

For all the color and life around her, though, Valentina felt alone. With no one to distract her, her thoughts kept coming back to Julián and her parents. She missed them so much.

Gradually, the earth shifted upward. Was she getting close to the canyon? Valentina took another look at the map to make sure she was on track, and her heart nearly stopped.

Her brother's *J* was no longer tucked away in Madremonte's castle. Instead, it blinked beside the Río de Lágrimas just north of her. He was close by! What did that mean? Had the queen let him go?

Valentina didn't think—she ran toward Julián.

The ground became slicker, with wide, flat rocks littering the path, and Valentina slipped more than once. Her legs burned as she focused on staying steady until finally, the terrain evened just as the river split into two branches. One stretched north, while the other curved sharply west, away from the mountains. A quick map check showed Julián's *J* blinking furiously on the branch that went west, as if saying, *What're you waiting for?*

That was the direction she took.

She didn't have to travel long. This branch of the river emptied into a lagoon surrounded by dense jungle. Mangroves grew around the far end, and there was more dirt, less sand. Giant lily pads that could probably hold her *and* her brother floated on its surface.

Valentina scanned the area. "Julián!" she called, not caring if anyone heard her. "Where are you?"

Something soft brushed against her cheek. A bright purple butterfly fluttered around her. Then came another, this one a deep pink. More butterflies joined them in blues and oranges.

They came in dozens, a rainbow of wings surrounding her.

Valentina backtracked, terror seizing her. There were so many she couldn't see where she was going. She flapped her hands and screamed until they finally flew away, into the trees.

And there, only a few feet away beside the lagoon, stood her brother.

"Julián!" Valentina ran to him and hugged him fiercely. A macaw's call echoed from somewhere up in the trees, but she barely heard it. All she could think of was her brother. He'd gotten free. Madremonte didn't have him anymore.

Julián squirmed free. "Stop it. I'm fine." He sounded tired.

Valentina held him at arm's length and studied him. He wore a straw hat she'd never seen before. His eyes were glassy, his cheeks flushed, and his arms hung limply at his sides, but other than that he looked unhurt. "Are you sure?"

"Yes."

"I was so scared," Valentina whispered. The ache Valentina had felt lessened. They were together again. He was safe. "What happened? Where's Doña Ruth?"

"Madremonte kept her." Julián didn't meet her gaze, and she had the sinking feeling the capybara was paying for helping them. When they got to the queen, Valentina would make sure to add freeing Doña Ruth to her requests.

"How did you escape? Are you hungry? Thirsty?" Valentina handed him a canteen, which he didn't take.

"No."

"Are you sure?" She frowned. "Where'd you get the hat?"

"Why so many questions?" Julián snapped.

His curtness stung. "Maybe because I've been worried and trying to get to you and I didn't know if you were okay." She sucked in a breath, trying to keep herself from crying. Attitude or not, her brother was safe. She was never, ever letting him out of her sight again, no matter how bratty he got.

"Everything is fine." Julián's hand jerked toward her, then fell to his side.

"Okay." Valentina wouldn't press him too much. He was probably tired. Who knew how long he'd journeyed or what conditions he'd been kept in? "What happened? How did you end up here?"

"Our queen is kind," Julián murmured. "She saw how much I missed you and let me come find you. I will bring you to her. Come with me."

Frowning, Valentina scanned their surroundings, but apart from the lagoon and the river, all she saw was a jungle full of darkness. "She's here?"

Julián laughed, though it sounded more like a forced cackle.

"Of course not. She doesn't leave her castle. But she knows you are lost and want to go home. She wants to help."

"How does she know I'm lost?" Valentina figured the queen had spies, but someone would have had to be monitoring Valentina's every move to know that she'd been separated from the duendes and stumbled onto this river on her own.

Valentina glanced at her brother. He hadn't replied. He stood rather still, as if in a trance. A nugget of dread started growing in her stomach. "Julián?"

"Yes?"

"How did she know I was lost?"

He shrugged.

Valentina paced, her feet kicking up dirt and rocks. It didn't make sense. Madremonte wouldn't just let Julián go, not after all the trouble of trying to drown them and sending el silbón. And how had Julián known where she was?

Something else bothered her. "How are we supposed to get to Madremonte's castle?"

"Through the river."

"What? How? We have no boat and no Albetroz."

"Swimming, of course."

"Swimming?" Valentina gaped at her brother. "Are you kidding me? The current of the river back there was strong. We can't swim in that. What did she do to you?"

"I'm fine." He reached out now and gripped her hand hard, crushing it.

"Ouch!" Valentina tried to pull away, but he held on tighter. "Let go, Julián. You're hurting me."

"Stop resisting. Just follow me."

With a strength she'd never seen him display, he started

dragging her toward the lagoon. Valentina yanked back, but he hung on.

"What's wrong with you?" Valentina screeched. "What are you doing?"

"I'm taking you to our queen."

Alarmed, Valentina dug her heels into the dirt and shifted her weight to counter him, but he kept hauling her toward the water.

Valentina spoke quickly, trying to regain control. "We'll drown! We can't go that way. We can walk to the castle." Valentina yanked again, harder this time, and managed to loosen his grip. She stumbled backward on the sand, the water just inches from her feet.

"I'll take care of you." Julián lunged for her legs, locking in around her ankles.

"No!" Valentina screamed, kicking. Madremonte must have done something to Julián's brain. This was her revenge.

Julián didn't react to her screams. He kept dragging her into the lagoon. Water trickled up her legs, wetting her back.

Dios mío. We're going to die!

Resistance wasn't working. She had to try something else.

Valentina went limp. Julián looked at her, half smiling. "That's a good girl," he murmured. "Madremonte will be pleased."

Then, with all the force she could muster, Valentina kicked hard. "Let. Me. Go!"

Julián stumbled into the lagoon, and Valentina broke free from his grip. She scampered back onto dry land, as far from the water as possible. Her little brother stood ankle deep in the lagoon, frowning. His hat floated away.

"Why did you do that, Valentina?"

This wasn't her little brother. It couldn't be.

Before she could answer, he reached toward her, and there, in the middle of his skull, was a huge hole the size of a guava.

THIRTY

Shock left her numb. What had the madremonte done to Julián? She stared at the gaping hole in her brother's head and shrank back, afraid he would try to grab her again.

"Stay away from me!" she yelled.

Instead of reaching for her, though, her brother twitched and then his *face* wrinkled and drooped, melting off like wax.

Valentina gasped. No—this was *not* her brother. This was some kind of monster.

She watched in horror as the creature's body stretched and Julián's brown skin faded to pink. Before her mind could grasp what she'd seen, the creature dove into the lagoon. She stared at the spot where it had disappeared until, suddenly, a pale pink dolphin jumped out of the water, twisting in the air before splashing back in and swimming away.

Was that . . . ?

Papi had told them stories about the Amazon pink dolphin. She stood, keeping her eyes on the lagoon as she sifted through what she remembered. These creatures were shape-shifters with magical powers. But none of the legends spoke of these river dolphins leading victims to watery deaths.

Of course, this wasn't the Amazon. This was Tierra de los Olvidados, and everything answered to the madremonte.

Anger rose in Valentina then, bright and crimson. Madremonte was heartless—no matter *what* Grucinda said. Grief had turned the queen into a monster.

"Why are you doing this?" Valentina screamed at the wind. She hoped whatever spies were out there would hear. "All I want is to go home with my brother to my family!"

Valentina fell to her knees. Her chest tightened.

"I hate you!" she yelled. "Papi was wrong. You're mean and cruel!" She hoped her words riled Madremonte so much the queen would come herself.

It took Valentina a few moments to hear the squeaking and splashing. She stared back at the lagoon, where the pink dolphin jumped and dove, as if trying to catch her attention.

"What?" Valentina snapped.

The dolphin squeaked again. Then, in a soft whisper, it said, "I won't hurt you."

Valentina scowled, staying far away from the lagoon's bank. "Why should I believe you?"

"I wasn't going to drown you," the dolphin said. "I was going to take you to her."

"By dragging me into the water?"

"You would have been safe," it insisted. "Asleep and protected, you would not have drowned. The queen does not want you dead."

Valentina snorted. "Yeah, right. That's why she sent the mohán to flush us out? Or el silbón to capture us?"

"She does not wish to kill you *yet*," the dolphin amended. "She wants to know who you are working for, how you broke through her enchantments, how you escaped her guards."

"That's a relief," Valentina said sarcastically.

The dolphin studied Valentina, the silence stretching between them. Finally, it said, "Your brother is alive."

Valentina's breath caught. "How do you know?"

"Because I saw him. I needed to study his countenance to take his shape."

Without another word, it jumped once more, diving into the river and swimming away.

"Wait!" Valentina called. "If Julián is in the castle, why did his *J* show up here?"

So many questions bubbled in her mind. Was the dolphin telling the truth? Could it still take her to Madremonte? Was Julián okay? But the dolphin disappeared beneath the water, and this time, it didn't return.

Valentina didn't get to dwell on it longer. A snap of a branch from the jungle made her whirl around. She peered into the trees, her feet firmly planted on the earth. It was impossible to see who—or what—was out there.

But there was something.

The hair on the back of her neck prickled with the sensation of being watched. Leaves rustled from different directions.

She raised her fists. "Who's there?" She'd never fought anyone, but she was done hiding.

The rustling stopped.

"Hello?"

Valentina steadied herself as the rustling and snapping started again, louder and faster. Whatever was out there was now barreling through the trees straight at her.

And she was ready.

Valentina pounced as two small creatures burst through the last trees. She didn't stop to question who or what they could be. The only thing going through her mind was *strike first, strike hard*. She ran at them, ready to knock the shorter one down, when she recognized the two braids and pointed hat.

"Isabella!" Valentina shifted at the last minute and landed sprawled on the ground.

"Vale!" the little duende squealed.

Valentina looked up to see Armando and Isabella peering down at her. Relief flooded every part of her like water rushing through a broken dam. She was so happy to see the two mischievous elves.

"You're okay!" Isabella said.

Valentina scrambled up, her face flushing. "Well, now I'm fine."

"We were worried," Armando said. "We're so sorry we ran ahead, and we figured you got lost and the Bosque was playing tricks on us—"

"So we had everyone looking for you," Isabella finished.

Valentina groaned. "Everyone?"

"Of course. We sent word to our Elders right away." Armando's expression turned serious. "We had a responsibility to get you to the mountains safely, so we had to find you."

Valentina felt a sudden rush of warmth toward them. They had kept their word, and they had gone out of their way to find her. When she got back home with Papi and Julián—*if* they got back home—she would make sure her father knew the legends had the duendes all wrong. "I'm so sorry."

"Us too," Isabella said. "We should've been more responsible."

Armando whistled sharply. A bright blue-and-yellow bird fluttered down to him. "Tell the Elders we've found her. Then tell Condor we're back to the original plan. We'll just be a couple hours late. Oh, and we'll be farther south."

"At least you're in one piece," Isabella said as the bird flew away.

"I know." After a pause, Valentina added, "But I almost wasn't." She told them about the pink river dolphin and almost getting dragged into the lagoon. "I don't even know how they were able to trick the map into showing Julián's *J* here instead of at the castle."

"Probably with Grucinda's magic," Isabella said. "Didn't you say the queen had taken her prisoner?"

Of course. Why hadn't Valentina thought of that?

Armando tugged on her arm. "I hate to break this party up, but we need to get going."

"Can we stick to the river?" Valentina asked.

Armando shook his head. "It's safer within the trees."

The duendes set off quickly, with Valentina at their heels. Gone was their earlier playfulness, and when they stayed close to her during their trek through the forest, she offered a silent thanks.

As they pushed north through the Bosque de Sueños, though, Valentina couldn't stop a thread of worry unraveling in her belly. Soon she would be at the madremonte's castle, and she had no idea what she would say or do.

Valentina's time was running out, and she had to come up with a solid plan—fast.

THIRTY-ONE

As dusk descended and light faded, so did the bright colors of the forest, but this only magnified the sounds from the shadows. An owl hooted. Cicadas chirred. Frogs croaked. And that same mournful wail she'd heard before pierced through the foliage. It was closer, and it filled Valentina with indescribable sadness. She felt an ache just like she'd felt before the earthquake.

Valentina remembered another legend. "Does la llorona live here, too?" The legend of la llorona told of a woman who roamed the countryside, weeping for her dead children.

"Nah," Isabella said. "The only crier we have is Madremonte. Every night, it's the same thing."

"She started the day her son disappeared," Armando said.

Despite her anger, Valentina couldn't help feeling sorry for the queen. Madremonte's world had been destroyed by humans, and then they took her only son. No wonder the queen hated them. No wonder she'd closed the borders. Why would she want to remain in the human world, protecting the earth, when all people did was cause her harm?

After a few more beats of silence, Isabella asked, "So what's the human world like?"

Valentina shrugged. "It's a lot like this one, I guess. Only we don't have duendes, witches, or dragons. And there's certainly no silbón or Madremonte. There's no magic."

"Then what *is* there?" Isabella asked.

"Well, there are mountains and rivers like here. My family's coffee farm is surrounded by both, and from our terrace, we can watch sunrises *and* sunsets. Our housekeeper, Doña Alicia, cooks amazing, and the coffee from our farm is the best in the world. That's what Papi says anyway. We have a creek nearby where we go to cool off on warm days," she said, thinking of it wistfully. "We do hear stories about you, but most people don't believe you exist."

"But we do!" Isabella exclaimed indignantly.

"I know," Valentina said softly. "So does my abuelo. And my dad. He has made it his mission to write all the stories down and find proof that they're true. That's why we were in the mountains when the earthquake hit. Why I ended up here."

Talking about Papi was like someone taking her heart in their fist and squeezing tight. Was he okay? Did he still have food and water? What if after all this, she failed? The thought filled her with a terror so deep and strong it knocked the breath from her.

"You'll save him," Armando said. "And your brother. I know you will."

Valentina couldn't answer. The alternative was too awful to consider.

They traveled through the night, and as the canopies above them began letting in dawn's lavender rays, Valentina knew they were close. They'd left the dense forest behind them, and she could see through the thinning trees the mountains ahead. The Bosque de Sueños had finally given up on confusing her. Maybe it had grown to like her, the way she had grown to like the duendes. They had done more than simply guide her as repayment for Valentina's help in the village. They'd kept her mind busy, made her laugh, come after her when she'd gotten lost.

They'd started to feel like friends.

"Will Condor be there, even with the detour?" she asked.

"He'll find us," Armando said. "We made sure of it."

So that was that. They were almost there. She would find her brother and get her chance to meet the queen who wanted them dead. This whole journey would come to an end.

It felt almost bittersweet, like a mango cut too soon.

The air turned cooler, zapping the lingering humidity, and the ground sloped upward. Valentina marveled at the shift that came with higher elevations. She felt a new burst of energy, and her pace quickened.

The whole be-kind, tell-the-truth plan felt weak, but she'd find her brother, and once reunited, they could come up with a better plan together. Maybe being in the castle would offer some clues that might help. She brought her fingers to her locket and Julián's crucifix, letting their presence comfort her.

Armando and Isabella hurried too, their steps quicker than they'd been through most of their trip. Soon they were barreling through the last trees.

Almost there.

Armando froze so suddenly Valentina almost toppled over him.

"What happened?" Isabella whispered, stepping closer to her brother.

The unmistakable sound of heavy breathing made the skin on Valentina's arms erupt in goose bumps. She'd heard this sound before—she was sure of it. She'd heard it in the Andes before the earthquake struck. Did that mean that someone from this world had been in Colombia—that the border wasn't as sealed as everyone thought? But that didn't make sense.

"We're not alone," Armando said.

Valentina peered around them, afraid of what she would see. Shrubs and dirt covered the ground. Tall, lean palms and oaks dotted their surroundings, along with a handful of shorter, wider palms. Her gaze settled on a quick movement to her right. There, hidden in the shadows, stood a woman smaller than the duendes. Long black hair draped around her body. Golden eyes bore right into Valentina. But it was her single leg that told Valentina exactly what creature they were dealing with.

"*That's* the patasola? The queen's guard?" She almost laughed.

Back at Grucinda's cottage, Patasola had certainly *sounded* much larger than the tiny creature before them now. Valentina and the duendes could easily outrun her. How had she captured the brujita?

"Yes," Isabella breathed.

"She doesn't look scary," Valentina said, though she couldn't deny the creature's golden stare was intimidating.

"Looks are deceiving, Vale," Armando said. The two duendes moved closer to Valentina until they almost touched.

"But she's so small."

As if in response, the patasola snarled at them, flashing razor-sharp teeth.

Valentina shrank back, but when the creature moved, it was to move *away* from them. She watched the patasola, confused. Not that Valentina was complaining, but why would the patasola retreat?

The answer came soon enough.

A large black boot sat at the foot of a palm tree. The tiny creature kept moving backward, then hopped into the boot. The earth began to rumble. Valentina stumbled, her jaw slack as she watched the patasola shoot out of the boot's opening, growing and stretching until she towered above them.

"RUN!" Armando yelled.

Valentina didn't need to be told twice. She took off after the duendes. They darted between trees and around bushes, trying to get as far away from their pursuer as possible. Valentina didn't dare look back, but she didn't need to. She heard the patasola crashing through the forest behind them.

Valentina charged on, trying to outrun Madremonte's guard.

THIRTY-TWO

"If Condor is there," Armando called over his shoulder, "he can take us. She can't fly."

Valentina's breathing quickened as the last tree came into view. They were going to make it. Armando and Isabella seemed to think the same, because suddenly, they ran even faster. Valentina grunted to keep up. Her legs burned and her feet ached, but she pushed herself more.

When she got home, she was never running again. Ever.

Behind her, twigs snapped. Against her better judgment, she looked back—and instantly wished she hadn't. The patasola had split herself into dozens of tiny patasolas that were gaining on them. Fast.

"Hurry!" Valentina screamed.

She'd escaped a flood, el silbón, and a shape-shifting dolphin. She wasn't about to be caught by another monster, not now when she was so close to reaching her brother and the castle. Valentina pumped her arms. *Faster!*

But then she tumbled as the miniature creatures jumped on her, clawing at her face. Valentina kicked and swiped, shrieking at the stabbing pain of their sharp teeth on her skin.

"Get off me!" She pushed off the ground, trying to get back up.

Every time she succeeded, more patasolas dragged her down. Rough hands jerked her arms behind her. Valentina cried out, wiggling to loosen their grip, but her strength was zapped. She couldn't do it. The tiny beings flew into action, securing her with a rope that seemed to materialize out of nowhere.

"No," Valentina groaned.

Armando and Isabella fell on the grass beside her. Their hair was matted and clothes tattered. Their straw hats lay scattered on the ground. Dirt smothered their features. They, too, were tied up.

"I'm sorry," Isabella whimpered.

"We should've sensed her," Armando said.

"It's not your fault," Valentina said. "It's mine." If she hadn't lost Armando and Isabella, they would've made it to the mountains earlier and they wouldn't be in this mess. She'd already be with Condor, flying to the castle, and the duendes would be back in their village, unharmed.

She'd messed everything up.

The tiny patasolas morphed once more into a single, terrifying being whose eyes shifted into a golden red. Like fire. Her long hair draped over her shoulders, and she wore a camouflaged tunic of leaves and moss cinched at the waist with vines.

"Let me go!" Valentina demanded.

Patasola hissed, revealing her sharp teeth. "Stupid human niña. Did you actually think you could outrun my daughters?"

Valentina tried to sit, wincing as the ropes cut even more into her skin. *Be kind.* The words flashed in her thoughts, but how could you be kind to a monster?

"Please. Take me to Madremonte."

The patasola scowled. "My queen will not give audience to a human. You are an intruder. Our queen does not always know what's best for this land, but she is correct in decreeing all humans must be dealt with in the harshest of manners."

Valentina couldn't breathe. "But she doesn't want me dead. The pink river dolphin told me so! Please. We didn't ask to come here. Our father was injured in an earthquake, which must've also opened the portal. She's the only one who can send me and my brother back to our world."

"Lies!" Patasola shrieked.

"I'm not lying!" Valentina said.

"The portal should've never been open between worlds," the patasola said. "Not then, not now. Look where it got our queen. I will deal with the flaws of the border's enchantments, just as I will deal with you and your brother."

"You can't do that!" Valentina said. "Madremonte wants me alive!" Desperation welled up inside her. "We're just two kids who want to go home. We haven't done anything wrong!"

"Her son was a child when he was taken," the patasola snapped. "My daughter was also a child when she disappeared in the human world. Many of our young were stolen by your kind. Human children become evil adults."

"We didn't hurt her *or* her land!" Valentina struggled again in her ropes. "We just want to go home."

The same bright blue-and-yellow bird from before perched on a branch above them. It whistled a few notes. Beside her, Armando straightened. Isabella nodded, then whistled a few notes back. Valentina felt a sliver of hope that maybe Condor was nearby. He could help them get out of this mess.

"QUIET!" The patasola lifted Valentina with one hand and the duendes with the other. The bird flapped away, taking all her hope with it.

Blinding sunlight washed over them, but it wasn't enough to warm the iciness spreading through her. "Where are you taking us?"

The patasola didn't answer.

"At least let the duendes go," Valentina choked out. "It's me you want."

"They are complicit. As are the capybara and witch. Oh, I told my queen as much—she should've never placed her trust in that bruja. Grucinda is probably the reason the portal opened—whether by accident or choice, it matters not."

Valentina felt her world tilt. "What did you do to them?"

"They'll never see the light of day again; though if you ask me, their treachery requires the worst of punishments. Alas, my queen deemed the dungeon to be fit."

Though Valentina knew Grucinda had likely been taken prisoner, the confirmation felt like a bucket of ice. And Doña Ruth. She hadn't even wanted to help them in the first place.

Valentina thought about Julián, sitting in a dungeon without knowing what had happened to her, probably scared and alone.

She would *not* let the patasola and madremonte win.

A plan began to form. She squirmed, shifting her body's weight from side to side. She felt herself swinging in the patasola's grip, and that gave her courage to keep struggling as hard as she could. If she could get loose, maybe she could untie herself.

It would be tricky, but she'd made it out of worse predicaments in this land.

"Stop that!" the patasola said.

"No!" Valentina wiggled even harder, even though every effort felt like a thousand needles plunging into her skin. "Not until you let me go!"

As if understanding her, the duendes started wiggling too. They worked themselves up so much that the patasola dropped the three of them on the prickly grass. Valentina rolled onto her back, the teal sky above her outlined with jagged mountain peaks. She struggled against the rope, trying to get loose, but it was useless.

The patasola loomed over Valentina, her eyes cooling into black holes. "You can take the rope off. It won't help you now."

With a single swipe of her clawed fingernails, the queen's guard sliced through the ropes.

Valentina jumped up, facing her. She lifted her fists up, ready to fight, even though her brain screamed that something wasn't right. Why would the patasola go through all the trouble of tying her up if she was just going to let her go?

The answer came a second later when, without warning, the queen's guard grabbed Valentina's shirt and pulled her close. "Your time is up, niña."

And she shoved Valentina off the cliff.

THIRTY-THREE

The wind snatched Valentina's scream as she tumbled in the air. Her chest tightened. Her stomach wedged in her throat. She couldn't breathe.

I'm dead. I'm dead. I'm dead.

Maybe her heart would stop thumping before she smashed into the ground. Maybe she'd pass out and not feel a thing. Maybe dying wouldn't hurt.

I don't want to die.

Valentina squeezed her eyes shut, as if by shutting out the whirling mountains around her, she could negate the fact that her body barreled toward the earth below.

Dios mío. Save me. Valentina couldn't even bring her hand to her face to do the sign of the cross, the way Abuelita had taught her to do in mass.

Then, just as suddenly, she wasn't falling any longer.

Her body jerked. A gasp escaped her lips. "What—?"

Tentatively, she moved her arms and legs. They swished through air. Her stomach settled back into place, even if the contents still sloshed around, making her queasy. She opened her eyes and found herself staring down into the canyon where she should've died, about a hundred feet below.

And she was rising.

Valentina shrieked and craned her neck. A large bird gripped her shirt with its sharp talons. Its black-and-gray wings spread wide above her. A soft white collar of feathers lined its neck, like the down of a winter coat. Condor! She would've recognized Colombia's national bird anywhere.

They coasted over the gorge, far away from the cliff and the patasola. Wind whipped her hair, stinging her cheeks.

She didn't care. She was alive!

As if sensing her gaze on him, Condor spoke. "Good day for a flight, don't you think?" His white curved beak and unsmiling, wrinkled face didn't match his light tone.

It took her a few beats to answer. "Lovely."

Condor shifted, and they soared toward the highest peaks of the Cordillera Monumental. Several of them jutted out against the blue sky, some still dotted with snow. Below them, the barren gorge held no river, only an endless carpet of dry, yellow grass.

"You know, when I told the Elders I would meet you in the Cañón de la Muerte, I did not think you would actually try to test its name."

Great. Another creature with a sense of humor. Valentina would be annoyed if she weren't so relieved. Condor had come for her, just as the duendes had promised. The bird they'd seen must have told him they were in trouble. The duendes had saved her life with all that whistling. "We have to go back for Armando and Isabella!"

"I'm afraid we can't do that," Condor said. They flew through two peaks onto another arm of the mountain range. For the briefest of moments, Valentina was reminded of the fins on Albetroz's back. She hoped he was okay.

"I managed to catch you before the queen's guard saw me." He glanced down at Valentina. "Going back would mean exposing that you didn't die, which means the queen would send her aerial legions. But as soon as I get you to safety, I will go back for them."

Valentina's heart sank, but she nodded. "She has guards in the air, too?"

"They only attack when given the order, so if they're not alerted, we'll be able to land safely at the top of the castle. It's quite high up and most of the guards are at the base."

Valentina didn't say more. Her thoughts churned in circles. She was back on track—and happy to be alive—but she couldn't help but worry about the duendes.

They flew in silence. After a while, Valentina noticed a structure in the distance nestled between two peaks. At first, it looked like a bridge suspended between them, but as they approached, she realized it was actually a castle poised over the canyon, connected to the mountains by two thin stretches of road. Its white-and-green facade reminded her of the churches back in Medellín. Gothic architecture, Papi told her once. Two towers rose high, topped with spikes. Buttresses curved out of the main structure, propping it up between the mountains, and stained glass windows dotted the exterior.

"Is that where we're going?" Valentina asked.

"Yes." Condor flew even higher. From this vantage point, the castle seemed to defy the laws of gravity.

He dipped then. Valentina felt the drop in her belly and cringed, wishing she could hold on to something or that they could land quickly. She didn't know how long the fabric of her T-shirt would hold.

"Please don't drop me."

Condor laughed, though it sounded more like a screech. He flew higher, then shifted right over one of the peaks until the building disappeared from sight.

"Wait, why are we going away from it?" She strained to glance back but couldn't. As relieved as she was that Condor had plucked her from the sky, she was ready to be on a firm structure.

"Can't let her see us coming," the bird replied.

He shifted once more, this time to the left to cross the mountain range again, and the sight left Valentina almost breathless. The towers they'd seen before were now directly below, their red barrel-tile roofs slanting downward like umbrellas. Between the towers lay an open courtyard with a small waterfall and lagoon, bright yellow flowering shrubs, and benches. An oasis within a castle.

And all around them, an abyss.

Condor settled Valentina atop one of the towers and landed next to her with a soft clank. Valentina shrieked as her feet slid on the slanted roof. Heart thudding in her ears, she sat quickly and dug her fingers into the tile grooves, which were covered with mold and dirt. But she didn't care. They were the only thing keeping her from sliding any farther. She didn't dare glance over the edge.

"Wouldn't inside the castle have been better?" she asked.

Condor chuckled. "Not without knowing where the queen is at the moment. Wait here. I'll be back." He flapped his great wings and left her perched on the rooftop, alone. She didn't have to wait long, though. Condor glided around the castle a few times before settling back next to her. "The queen is in her throne room. This tower is guarded, but the other is not. That will be your entry point."

He flew off with her once more, then landed on the balcony of the other tower.

"This door will lead you down to the upper levels, which includes the bedchambers," Condor said. "You must take care not to be spotted by anyone—guard or servant—on your way down. However, from my flyover, it looked as though all the guards were with Madremonte in the throne room, and the servants were in the kitchens."

Avoid the throne room and kitchens—check. "Do you know where the dungeon is?"

"On the bottom level, two stories below the throne room. But take great care. There's no knowing what our queen will do should she find you in her home."

Valentina had a pretty clear idea of what the madremonte might do. "It doesn't matter. I need to get my brother and talk to her. We need to go back home and save my father." Her fingers curled around Julián's crucifix and the locket hanging from her neck.

Condor bowed his head. "Good luck, señorita. I wish you well."

"Gracias. I'll need all the luck you can give."

THIRTY-FOUR

Condor spread his wings wide and flew off the roof, leaving Valentina alone once more. She stood there for a few moments, watching him grow smaller and smaller until he disappeared between mountain peaks.

Let's do this.

She fumbled through a glass door and tumbled into the tower. Little sunlight pierced the dimness in this space, but as her eyes adjusted, she realized it was enough to move around. Her gaze landed on a pair of figures guarding the door into the castle, and she jumped, holding in a yelp. Upon closer inspection, though, she saw they were just suits of armor—oddly shaped ones, with horns and spiky shells and long alligator snouts.

There was nothing else in the room except for a tapestry that covered an entire wall. She realized it was an enormous map of Tierra de los Olvidados, much like the one Grucinda had given her—only twenty times larger and more colorful. She approached it slowly, and her fingers traced over the oceans to the east and west. She found the Río de Mil Colores and Río de Lágrimas, among others. She saw plains and forests and mountains. Even a rainforest. This world truly was a flip-flopped image of Colombia—with some exceptions, of course.

But what grabbed her attention the most was the image of the madremonte in the middle. Here, the queen knelt as if in prayer, arms held high, black hair sweeping over the floor. She wept tears of gold, which ran down her cheeks into a puddle that covered everything near her. Surrounding her were the patasola, silbón, and mohán, as well as other creatures Valentina had yet to meet. Their heads were bowed, their hands over their chests.

In the corner of the tapestry, away from the queen and her people, was a baby. A golden halo surrounded his indistinguishable features, and a row of humans separated him from the rest of the magical land.

Madremonte's son.

Valentina's fingers paused on the baby's tuft of brown hair. Her chest tightened. A deep sorrow emanated from this tapestry, so strong it took her breath away. She shook herself, tearing her eyes from the image. She couldn't get distracted. She had a dungeon to find. Silently, she tiptoed toward the door, the weight of the scene still heavy over her.

Condor had said the dungeon was two stories below the throne room. But he hadn't said how many floors were in the castle.

Only one way to find out.

Valentina pushed the door open. It groaned, low and insistent, and she froze, holding her breath. No footsteps rushed toward her. No guards shouted at her to halt. In front of her was a long, narrow hallway lined with lit torches. At the end of the hallway, there was another closed door, and beside it, a staircase going down.

Valentina ignored the door and went to the stairs. She had to keep making her way toward the dungeon, toward her brother and the others who'd been locked up because of her.

Her mochila felt heavy on her shoulders as she reached the end of the staircase, landing in the center of another hallway. Her feet barely made a sound on the carpet, which she realized was made of tightly woven grass. Portraits lined the walls, interrupted only by a few doors. Most of the doors stood open, so she peeked in each one, hoping to find the throne room to guide her. Instead, she discovered a series of plain bedrooms decorated with nature: canopies made of leaves on four-poster oak beds; vines dotted with tangerine flowers woven into bedspreads; slabs of stone piled up in the shape of armoires, with pale pink orchids as decoration. In one room, she found a library lined with books of all sizes. A reading nook was carved out of the rock, above which lay a wide window overlooking the surrounding mountains.

Something about it all gave her a fuzzy feeling of déjà vu. The castle felt like an oddly familiar song, one you knew you'd heard but couldn't quite place your finger on when or where. Like a memory from a dream. Was this part of Papi's stories?

Valentina couldn't remember, and she didn't have time to wonder.

When she was certain the throne room wasn't on this level, she headed back toward the staircase. She hesitated for a moment, listening for footsteps or any other sound that warned of incoming guards. Her gaze swept over the hallway and the portraits until it landed on the one right beside her.

And what she saw made every hair on her arms stand up.

"Papi?" Valentina whispered.

She forgot where she stood and her purpose. All she could do was stare at the life-sized portrait of her father hanging in this castle. As if it belonged there. Valentina squeezed her eyes shut and opened them again. There he was, smirking at her as if saying, *What did you expect?* She studied the painting carefully. He must've been about three in the painting, his face a smidge darker than it usually was, like the glow that comes with endless days in the sun. And his large brown eyes shone bright with his signature *I know something you don't* look.

Julián's look.

It reminded her of another image. Valentina slipped the locket from under her shirt and twisted it open. Staring back at her was her father's face, a little older here. With a start, she remembered what he'd told her when he'd given her the necklace. *This is the youngest picture there is of me. I don't have any from when I was a baby.*

And yet here he was. Younger.

How could this be? What was Papi's painting doing *here*?

Valentina tucked the locket back under her shirt and pressed her fingers against the bumpy canvas, willing it to speak. She tried to pull together the threads of information she'd gathered throughout her journey. Humans had been in this land a long time ago, *hundreds* of years before the queen closed the border. Time moved differently here. Could it be that Papi had come in then, had walked through the same lands Valentina had just trekked through? But he'd never mentioned it, and neither had her abuelitos. If Papi had come as a child, he would've said something, right?

And even if Papi had visited, why would Madremonte hang his picture in the castle?

Something didn't add up.

Valentina stepped aside, staring at the other images now. Most of them were of adults wearing crowns of leaves and robes of moss, though there were a couple children aside from her father—a golden-skinned girl about Valentina's age, a little girl with wild dark hair, and a scowling teenage boy with mossy-green eyes.

Her gaze snagged on another image. Beside her father hung a portrait of a woman with sharp features and a piercing gaze. She sat on a golden throne, back straight, chin high, hands on her lap. Madremonte.

On her right cheek, a cluster of freckles shone like stars on her dark skin.

With a gasp, Valentina brought her hand to her own cheek, where a similar set of freckles sat. She had *never* met anyone with this pattern—Abuelito always said they meant she was a star, a princess. That no one on earth had them. But here was a portrait of Madremonte with the same freckles on the same cheek.

She turned back to Papi's portrait. A gleam of light on gold caught her attention, as her gaze settled on a small plaque below the painting.

MARCOS, BELOVED SON. MISSING SINCE LA GRAN VIOLENCIA.

And everything Valentina had ever known imploded.

THIRTY-FIVE

Papi was Madremonte's long-lost son.

Valentina and Julián were her grandchildren!

If she thought about it, it all made sense. Madremonte's son was five when he'd been kidnapped. Papi's earliest picture was exactly at that age. He believed in magic, in legends and stories that according to everyone were make-believe but which were real for him. He could've only known all this if he'd actually lived here, right?

Valentina reeled with this revelation. It didn't matter that Papi's name was Ricardo, not Marcos. He must've changed his name at some point. And he did always say his younger years were filled with "gran violencia" from cartels and guerrillas. But why hadn't he told them? Why hadn't her abuelitos said anything about Papi being adopted—and how in the world did the queen's kidnapped son even end up with her abuelitos? They claimed Papi's early photographs had been lost in a house fire, but they had to be lying.

The portrait in this castle was proof.

Then another thought occurred to her: This must be why Valentina felt the premonition before the earthquake and before the flood, the uneasiness at the earth being unhappy. Because she was the madremonte's granddaughter. Was that why she and Julián had gotten through the portal, too? Because they were the queen's descendants? Maybe the patasola was wrong, and it had nothing to do with Grucinda.

So many more questions barreled through her mind, but she didn't have time right now.

She had to find her brother.

And then she had to find Madremonte—her grandmother.

For the first time since setting off to find the queen, Valentina knew what she would offer her in exchange for their safety and for saving their father.

A crash from above pulled her away from the painting. Valentina tensed, her heart thudding so loud she thought the entire castle could hear it. When no one came, she darted down the stairs toward the next level. Right now she needed to focus on finding her brother. He needed her, and somewhere in their world—the *real* world—Papi needed them.

Everything else would have to wait.

She gripped the banisters and flew down another flight, taking the steps two at a time. She didn't stop to look at anything else—she couldn't bear more surprises. Three flights down, Valentina paused briefly to catch her breath. Next to the stairs stood a closed pair of wooden double doors with two brass bolts, both shaped in the same upside-down *V* and circle that she'd seen at the entrance to Tierra de los Olvidados. From behind it, she heard angry shouts followed by a loud bang, as if someone were hitting a table.

"Silence!" yelled a woman inside.

A chilly stillness followed, and Valentina tensed. Murmurs continued then, and she caught fragments of "human" and "unbelievable" and "she'll come."

They knew she'd survived the fall.

But also—she'd found the throne room! Which meant the dungeon was two more levels down.

She hurried down the remaining floors.

The stairs spilled onto a tight corridor lit by torches, which cast an orange glow on the stone walls. Shadows wavered and elongated, creating an eeriness worthy of Papi's legends.

Small doors with barred windows broke up the monotony of the limestone. Valentina counted more than a dozen—and that was only what she could see before the hallway curved. She hoped it wouldn't take too long to find Julián. She couldn't call out his name, not if she wanted to keep her presence a secret.

Valentina started with the cell closest to her. The barred windows were barely reachable on her tippy toes, so she curled her hands around the bars and boosted herself up.

Empty.

She moved on to the following door, which held a horned creature she didn't recognize. She ducked back down before it could see her and continued to the next door. And the next. She found duendes, a tapir, and another patasola, this one seemingly less vicious than the queen's guard. She lifted her red-rimmed eyes toward Valentina, a silent plea on her face.

Who were they? What crimes had they committed against a queen who suspected everyone of treason, who had spies and guards everywhere?

What kind of monster had her heartbroken grandmother turned into?

Valentina kept moving through the dungeon, a sudden, sickening thought hitting her: What if Julián was in the throne room? Or worse—what if the queen had already executed him?

No. Valentina would search every crevice of this castle before giving up hope.

Before the hallway's curve, Valentina found Doña Ruth curled on a tuft of hay. Her fur was matted and caked with mud. As Valentina watched, the capybara whimpered a short, shrill bark, her ears flicking.

"Doña Ruth," Valentina called softly.

The capybara startled to her feet, pressing herself against the walls. When their gazes met, Doña Ruth's eyes widened.

Valentina held a finger to her lips, and the capybara nodded, ambling toward the door on an uneven gait. "Are you okay?"

"I have been better, but I'm alive." Her eyes glistened.

"I'm going to get you out."

Doña Ruth shook her head. "Find your brother. I do not deserve your kindness. He is two doors down."

Valentina shook her head. "I'm not leaving you."

"My child, do not make this harder. Just know that I am truly sorry."

"For what?"

Tears dribbled down the fur on her snout. Valentina could barely hear her when she said, "It was my fault our queen knew you were by the river, my fault the flood happened."

"You?" Valentina's heart sank. She'd been so sure it was Don Babou. She had trusted Doña Ruth—albeit reluctantly. "But why?"

"I was afraid. We're under strict orders," Doña Ruth said. "Should a human cross into our world, we are to turn it in. I was following the rules. Not even Don Babou gave you away, even if he thought Don Pedro a fool. I'm a traitor," she wailed.

Valentina pressed her lips together. That flood cost them time, gave Madremonte a location, and from there, it would've been easy to spy on them. Even with the mano peluda's screeching, they might have made it to the castle sooner, and together, had the capybara not alerted the queen.

"We've always been told humans are evil," Doña Ruth continued. "They hurt our land and people. They took Madremonte's only son, probably killed him."

If you only knew. Valentina felt the urge to tell her about Papi, about the truth Valentina had just uncovered. But no, she would hold this secret tight until she met with the queen.

The element of surprise would deliver them. It had to.

Even though Doña Ruth had betrayed them, she sat in a rank cell, branded as a criminal like the others here. "Why are you locked up?" Valentina asked.

"Because I tried to keep your brother away from el silbón. You have to believe me. By the time I realized you were not the evil human we'd been warned about, it was too late."

"I see." Would Valentina have done the same thing as the capybara in the same circumstances? Maybe. Hadn't she judged everyone on this land, too? Valentina searched for a spark of anger, but only an aching emptiness lingered. Nothing would be okay until she found her brother, until they got back home and saved Papi. "What's done is done. I'm going to get Julián and you out."

Without waiting for the capybara to reply, Valentina dashed toward the door that would hold her brother. Sure enough, when Valentina pulled herself up to peer into the window, she saw him lying in a corner beside a second barred window, the only source of natural sunlight in the cramped cell. His jeans had ripped in some spots. His shirt was splattered with dirt and mud. Twin angry gashes peeked from his knees, and his hair stuck out all over. Otherwise, though, he seemed unhurt.

"Julián," Valentina whispered.

He didn't turn around. A soft murmur of a melody reached her, and Valentina realized he was humming the song Mami used to sing to them when they were little. Tears welled in her eyes.

"Julián!" Valentina called again, louder this time. Her voice bounced off the stone walls. She cringed, but the moment her brother turned and his scared eyes met hers, she no longer cared.

Julián scrambled up from his makeshift bed and ran toward the door. "Vale! I thought you'd never come!"

"Shhh, I'm here. I'm going to get you out."

"But it's locked!"

"I'll figure something out."

Just then, Valentina heard a low, deep whistle that sounded far, far away. Her skin crawled in response. She knew that whistle very well.

Slowly, she turned around, coming face-to-face with el silbón and la patasola.

THIRTY-SIX

Valentina didn't run this time. She stood with her shoulders back and chin up, like Madremonte in her portrait. From behind the door, she heard Julián whimper, and she curled her hands in anger. No one made her brother cry—*no one*.

"Let him out," Valentina said.

"Insolent child." The patasola started toward her. When Valentina didn't cower in fear, she paused. Beside the patasola, el silbón flashed his razor-sharp teeth.

Nope. Valentina wouldn't be intimidated so easily now. She pushed down the shiver threatening to rise. "Let him out," she repeated. "And take us to your queen. Now."

"Why should we listen to a human girl?" el silbón rasped.

"Because I know where her son is."

He winced, his leathery forehead wrinkling. "We don't speak of the young master." He almost seemed afraid.

"Why should we believe you?" the patasola sneered, though her voice trembled slightly.

Valentina studied the two. As scary as they were, they still reported to Madremonte. She had a feeling that if they messed up, the queen would show little sympathy toward them.

"I should dispose of you right here," the patasola said. "Finish what I started." El silbón placed a hand on the patasola's arm, and she scowled at him.

Valentina shrugged, trying to seem indifferent. "If you don't let my brother out and take us to your queen, and I'm telling the truth, then you've just cheated her from finding her son. How do you think she'll thank you for that? If I'm lying, then she'll kill me anyway."

"Very well," el silbón said. "We'll play your little game. But if you're lying—" He jabbed a bony finger in her face. "I will be the first to enjoy watching your lie combust." He stepped around Valentina and unlocked the door.

Julián stumbled out of his cell and into Valentina's arms. She hugged him tightly. He was really there. He was alive.

"Move it." The patasola pushed Valentina and Julián forward.

Hands clasped tight, they followed el silbón out of the dungeon. Patasola brought up the rear. When they passed Doña Ruth's cell, Valentina fought the urge to ask them to let her go too. She didn't think they would indulge her any more.

She'd have to wait until she convinced Madremonte of the truth. That they were her *grandchildren*. Valentina's fingers touched the lump of the locket beneath her T-shirt, still not quite believing how incredible this discovery was.

"Do you really know where her son is?" Julián whispered.

"Yes." She didn't dare tell him more. He'd just have to find out when she revealed it to the queen.

They climbed the stairs to the next floor and stopped before the wooden double doors of the throne room. Up close, Valentina could see the oak's rich grain and deep, earthy browns. Slivers of light stretched along the hallway before them, coming from open windows at each end.

"Wait here, and don't get any bright ideas," el silbón warned, before disappearing behind the doors. The shouting inside the throne room stopped.

"I see your bluff, niña," the patasola growled behind her. "I'll let you play your game, and then I will take great pleasure in destroying you."

Valentina stayed silent, staring ahead. Beside her, Julián gripped her hand tighter.

After what felt like forever, the doors opened. El silbón reappeared and jerked his head toward the room. "Go on. Her Majesty is waiting for you."

Valentina took a deep breath and walked in. She kept her chin up, but her brother maintained his gaze on the floor. It took all the restraint she had not to hold him the way she used to do when he was a toddler and he got scared or hurt. There was no time for comfort.

It was the moment of truth.

The interior of the throne room was massive. Valentina had to crane her neck to see the vaulted ceiling, which rose dozens of feet in the air and glittered like a night sky full of stars. Floating chandeliers of carved driftwood gave off a soft, shimmering glow. Pale green vines curled and uncurled against the gray walls.

Valentina exhaled, scanning the room. A group of creatures sat as still as stone at a long bamboo table. She recognized a few of them from Papi's stories. The cura sin cabeza, a headless priest with long black robes. The muelona, a woman with an electrifying gaze, long dark hair, and a mouthful of terrifying sharp teeth. The hombre caimán, a creature that had the body of an alligator and the face of a man. An older woman surrounded by fire who could only be the candileja.

"You."

Valentina's attention snapped to the woman behind the stern voice. In the center of the room, gripping the armrests of her throne, was the madremonte.

The queen's bright, glowing eyes bored into them. They

reminded Valentina of a golden flame. Madremonte definitely didn't look like Valentina's abuelita back home, whose gray bun and soft skin invited comfort. This grandmother inspired awe and fear. She sat with the same rigid back she had in the portrait. Tension rippled from her. Her dark hair fell over her shoulders down to her waist, like waves of a river. A robe of moss and periwinkle wildflowers clung to her skin, and a crown of leaves and pink orchids lay on her head. Golden bangles snaked around her arms, and, on her right hand, an emerald ring gleamed.

The portal!

The patasola and silbón bowed before the queen, and when Valentina and Julián didn't, the two guards pushed them down. Cold stone bit through Valentina's jeans.

"Rise." Madremonte's voice boomed against the walls.

Valentina did as commanded, pulling her brother up. She lifted her gaze to meet the queen's, and the moment their eyes locked, her confidence wavered. Her plan hinged on Madremonte listening and believing what Valentina had to say.

What if, after all this, she wouldn't?

"Come forward," the queen ordered.

No one spoke. Even the guards stood silently.

Valentina took a few steps toward the queen, but Julián held back. She couldn't blame him. After hearing about the madremonte's wrath throughout their journey, and after surviving the mohán, silbón, and river dolphin, Valentina had developed a healthy dose of apprehension. She tried to keep herself from shaking, but the most she managed was not melting into a puddle on the floor.

Madremonte watched them like a predator studying prey. Valentina tried to find her voice, to say what she needed to, but the words *We know where your son is!* stuck to the roof of her mouth.

She gaped at the woman who was her grandmother but didn't know it.

"You have trespassed on these lands forbidden to your kind," Madremonte said with the authority of judge and executioner. "You corrupted my people."

She waved to the left, and Valentina's heart sank when she saw what she'd missed before: Armando and Isabella in chains made of vines, standing beside the long table.

"You escaped my most experienced guards," the queen continued. "And here you are, demanding to see me. Who do you think you are?"

Valentina opened her mouth, then closed it. It was now or never. She searched inside for a strength she didn't feel and blurted, "We're your grandchildren."

THIRTY-SEVEN

Deafening silence met Valentina's announcement. She held her chin high, shoulders squared. She didn't dare glance at Julián to see his reaction. She only had eyes for her grandmother.

The queen's chest rose and fell as her hands gripped the armrests so tightly, Valentina thought they'd break into pieces. Beneath the glow of the chandeliers, the emerald stone on her finger glittered.

"What?" Julián murmured beside her.

Valentina flinched. Maybe not telling him had been the wrong decision.

Around the table, the creatures burst into agitated murmurs. In the other corner, Isabella and Armando stared at her in shock. A sharp wind kicked up, and the vines clinging to the walls shifted. Valentina struggled to keep the dread inside her from rising.

"It's true," she said loud enough for all to hear, keeping her gaze on the madremonte. "I didn't know until I came here, but our papi is your son, and he's in trouble. If we don't get to him soon, he's going to die."

"Lies!" Madremonte shot up from her throne, stretching until she towered above them, almost three times as tall.

A gust of wind roared toward Valentina, knocking her down. She scrambled back up, balled her fists, and yelled, "It's the truth!"

Someone at the long table gasped. Valentina didn't turn to see who it was. She kept her gaze on the queen. Maybe she was being defiant, but she didn't care. Madremonte needed to know where her son was. Valentina and Julián needed to get home.

Those two absolutes wove together into a tapestry of their own.

"We came here to ask you to send us home," Valentina said. "To help us save him. He doesn't have much longer. You can see him for yourself if you help us."

"Silence!"

The word ricocheted against the walls, springing the vines free. They grew longer, reaching toward Valentina and Julián. The wind intensified too, snapping at them like a whip.

Doubt crept over Valentina. What if the truth wasn't enough?

The room erupted into screams as the creatures at the table scraped back their chairs and darted toward the exit. Julián gripped Valentina's hand hard.

"Vale?" he asked.

Behind her, el silbón hissed, "Why would you say that?"

The patasola growled, "It's your funeral."

Before Valentina could reply, the two guards bowed and fled with the others. The doors barely made a sound when they shut, not with the roar of the wind and the anger unfurling from Madremonte.

"You thought you would make fun of my pain?" the queen thundered.

Fire spewed from her eyes. Her voice deepened, and she threw her arms in the air, curling her fingers. As if in response, rain began to fall from the ceiling. The vines multiplied, crawling into all the empty spaces. They sprouted leaves, which shot out more vines. Over and over, the cycle continued beneath the rain.

She's going to crush us.

Valentina fought the urge to flee. It wouldn't work. Madremonte would follow. Besides, running away wouldn't convince her to send them home, to save Papi.

The only way to succeed was to keep talking until the truth clicked.

"My father, your *son*, told me stories about you," she yelled, trying to make her voice heard above the howl of the wind. "You were always good and kind in them, protecting your land above everything else. And I know inside you're still like that. What those humans did to you when they stole your son—that was horrible. But you're a good woman. You have to be. You're my grandmother."

Rain poured down in torrential sheets, the kind that flooded rivers and destroyed life. Valentina wiped the drops from her eyes. Already, water pooled at her feet.

"When we got here, I had no idea where we were. And everyone we met kept telling us how *odd* it was that we got through a border that *you* closed and that only *your* magic could open. And then I kept seeing things that I had only heard about in Papi's stories or in his books. He'd captured Tierra de los Olvidados so perfectly. I thought it was his imagination, but all this time, it must have been because he remembered this world. His home."

Wind howled in agony. Hail pelted Valentina's skin.

"Vale, what are you doing?" Julián said. "She's going to kill us!"

"I saw a painting of Papi here, in her castle! It said it was a painting of the prince!"

"ALL LIES!" the queen cried, and thunder rang throughout the room. "Human children become evil adults." The words were eerily familiar. The patasola had spoken them before pushing Valentina off the cliff. "You circumvented my rules and poisoned my land, and now you are spreading falsehoods. You will be punished!"

"I am *not*!" Valentina screamed. She pushed herself to keep going. "I couldn't understand why Papi's stories were so magical. I couldn't understand his fascination with you. Do you know that he wrote about you the most?"

Water rose to Valentina's knees, as if contained by an invisible box. She forced herself to keep talking, even though her teeth had begun chattering. Madremonte had to see the truth.

If she didn't, they were as good as dead.

"We were in the mountains back home when an earthquake hit. Papi fell through a crack in the earth, and we couldn't get him out. He was hurt. Then we fell too, and found the entrance to the portal. Do you know that the boulder blocking the cave rolled away on its own? Like magic? We'd barely touched it when it moved. And when we entered, it shut us in. That's how we got here. I don't know exactly how or why. All I know is that Papi is lying hurt, and if we don't get back soon, he's going to die!"

"STOP IT!" Madremonte pressed her hands against her ears, like Julián did when he was done listening to his sister. Then the queen spread her hands wide, and vines shot forward. Valentina reacted automatically, pulling Julián against her.

"Look at the freckles on my cheek!" she yelled. "They're just like yours!"

But the vines reached them anyway, and wrapped around their ankles. Panic engulfed Valentina, sent her heart thumping so fast she thought it would burst through her chest.

The queen wasn't listening. If only Valentina could show her . . . the locket!

"I can prove it!" She yanked off her chain and threw it at Madremonte's feet. "There's a picture in there of my father, a little older than the painting hanging on your wall. But it's the same boy—your son."

A beat. Two. Four.

Valentina held her breath as the queen seemed to consider, the expression on her face warring between eagerness and anger and fear. Finally, she lowered her hands. The wind quieted down, the rain slowed to a sprinkle. Even the vines paused, as if awaiting orders.

Tentatively, Madremonte picked up the locket by the chain. She stared at it as if it might bite her and, with shaking hands, unlocked it.

The wail that came from the queen rippled out in pure, undiluted pain. It was the same sound Valentina had heard in her nights across Tierra de los Olvidados. She felt her grandmother's pain in the depths of her heart, an ache much stronger than that before the earthquake. And she knew without a doubt that the queen saw what Valentina had seen.

Madremonte fell to her knees, her face wet—not from the rain she'd conjured but from the tears that flowed like a newly fed spring.

Around them, water receded. Vines shrank back into decorations on the walls. Wind disappeared. The only proof that anything out of the ordinary had happened was in the overturned chairs and in the puddles scattered throughout the floor, where Madremonte now rocked, cradling the locket against her chest.

And there, barely audible in the great room, the queen choked out, "My son."

THIRTY-EIGHT

Julián's breathing tickled her arm, but Valentina didn't dare move. She was afraid if she shifted in the slightest, the spell would be broken and Madremonte would turn on them again.

Finally, after what felt like years, the queen stood and approached them. She'd shrunk back to her normal size. Her eyes shone brightly, and the lines on her face softened. On her cheek, the cluster of freckles flickered like stars.

The queen smiled at them. Kind. Benevolent. Nothing like the monster they'd seen moments earlier.

Valentina returned the smile tentatively, though inside, her emotions warred. The madremonte had tried to drown them, had inflicted so much pain on her land. On her people. Valentina didn't know if she could forgive her. But then she remembered her own fear, helplessness, and anger when Julián had been taken and when Papi had fallen into that crevice. She would've stopped at nothing to save them.

Maybe people and legendary beings responded to grief in similar ways.

"Your father . . . my son?" The queen's voice held all the wonder of her kingdom and Valentina's world combined. "How?"

"I don't know," Valentina said. "He gave me that locket when I was little and I didn't want to go to school. I was afraid I'd forget what he looked like, so he gave it to me so I could always remember."

"He sounds like a wonderful father," Madremonte said.

"He is." Valentina ached for him—for his eccentricities and tales, for his persistence in documenting the legends, for his clove-scented hugs when she was scared, for his unconditional love.

After one last glance at the picture, Madremonte snapped the locket shut and pressed it into Valentina's hand. Her touch was warm, gentle. "Thank you." She turned to Julián, ruffling his hair. "And you."

He glared at the queen.

Our grandmother. Valentina didn't know if she'd get used to this new fact.

"You both exhibited tremendous courage to come here, to risk everything I sent your way. I am truly sorry." She sighed, looking past them to the doors of the throne room. "When my son vanished, I swore those responsible would pay. I swore to protect this land, to cut off that which was diseased and broken. To do so, I had to seal the border. No ordinary human would have been able to break that barrier, and neither could most of the beings here. Only my guard Patasola had access to your world, to search for my son. I believed her when she said that Grucinda had meddled with the portal, but I should have known better."

Valentina remembered the sound of heavy breathing that she'd heard first in the Andes and again when Patasola had found her and the duendes. *So Patasola* was *in the mountains before the earthquake!* Then Valentina processed the rest of the queen's words. "Wait, so the droughts, earthquakes, and eruptions back in my world—you made them happen?"

Madremonte closed her eyes and shook her head. "Not quite. In closing the border, I decided to leave humans to their own self-destructiveness as a punishment for stealing my son. Without my presence there, it would be a matter of time before the earth would do the rest. It's a living being, keenly aware of the care it's given, and it is always trying to maintain a balance. Those disasters you speak of are the land's way of fighting for breath when it's being choked by insatiable greed."

Julián scowled. "Then it's because of *you* Papi got hurt and we ended up here."

Pain filled the queen's face. "I'm so sorry, more than you can imagine. I assumed our world would be safer this way as long as my own portal existed, the last connection between two worlds, which are intertwined the way twins might be." She met their gazes now, pleading. "I was wrong."

Julián opened his mouth to protest, but Valentina shook her head. Right now, they had to focus on getting back home to their father.

"Papi didn't have much food or water left," she told Madremonte. "I don't even know if the ledge he's on held up. We've already wasted too much time trying to get here."

The queen held up her hand. "Say no more. We will save your father—my son." She pressed a hand against her chest again.

"We?" Valentina asked.

"You don't expect me to learn my son is still alive and not go after him myself, do you?"

"Well, no, but I thought you never left this land?"

Madremonte laughed, and as she did, the shadows of the throne room cleared. A brilliant light shone above them from skylights that had been hidden before, bathing the space in a rose gold. She strode to the double doors and threw them open. "Sofía! Rafael!"

"I don't like this," Julián muttered out of earshot. "That's not even Papi's name."

"It's the truth," Valentina said. "Besides, what matters right now is getting to Papi."

Her brother grunted and crossed his arms. Seconds later, the patasola and silbón appeared. It was all Valentina could do not to dissolve in giggles. The imposing guards had names as ordinary as hers.

"Yes, my queen," they said in unison.

"Get yourselves and the others ready. We will be paying the human world a visit."

"Isn't that dangerous for you?" Rafael said, gaping at her as if she'd lost her mind. "Humans—"

"Not this time. My grandchildren—and my son—need me." She turned to Valentina and Julián and beamed.

Sofía's head swiveled between them. A vein bulged on her throat and her jaw clenched. She glared at Valentina before returning her attention to the madremonte. "Your Highness. This is a trick. We searched everywhere for young Marcos—"

"Which makes me wonder how hard you truly searched. If you had, you'd have found him." There was a dangerous edge in their grandmother's voice, and the patasola flinched. So did Julián. Valentina would have been freaking out too, if she hadn't known the madremonte was on their side.

"We have proof," Valentina said, and with a smirk, showed Sofía the locket.

The patasola glowered. "The child could have found this. It doesn't mean anything."

"This image was taken *after* Marcos's disappearance," the queen shot back.

Sofía didn't budge. "He disappeared over three hundred years ago. There's no way these two children could be his offspring. We saw what treachery humans were capable of during La Gran Violencia. For all we know, this child is working against you with Grucinda. I always said that witch was the one to blame."

That snagged something in Valentina's memory.

The duendes had said someone on this land had helped the humans who'd kidnapped the prince. And Albetroz had told them that the patasola blamed the brujita, though she couldn't prove it. Then there was Grucinda, who didn't trust the patasola.

There were many rumors going around—but who had started them?

Valentina narrowed her eyes at Sofía, all the pieces of the invisible puzzle snapping into place, including what the patasola had said right before throwing Valentina off the cliff: *Our queen does not always know what's best for this land. . . . The portal should've never been open between worlds. Not then, not now.*

"It was you," Valentina said slowly. "You took Marcos away. You gave him to humans. It's your fault the borders closed."

THIRTY-NINE

Sofía roared, lunging at Valentina, who shrieked and darted out of reach. Julián, as if spurred on by the attack, raised clenched fists and screamed, "Stay away from my sister!"

Valentina had never wanted to hug him more. But there would be time for that later. She tugged him away from the guard and shoved him toward the doors.

"Hide," she hissed.

"No!" Julián said. "I'm not getting separated from you again. We fight together."

Together. Yes, the two of them could handle anything as long as they were together.

Rafael stepped in front of them, and Valentina braced herself for his attack. Instead, she was surprised when he turned and faced the patasola. "Easy, Sofía," he said, as if trying to calm a spooked animal. "Remember yourself."

The patasola shoved him out of the way, spitting out, "Filthy. Humans. All they do is take and take until there's nothing left." She closed in on Valentina.

Before Sofía could reach her, though, Madremonte bellowed, "STOP!" Vines shot out from her raised hands and wrapped around the patasola.

"You will not lay a hand on my grandchildren." The queen's voice was dangerously low.

Sofía struggled against the vines, but it was clear she wasn't going anywhere.

Madremonte approached, her face contorted in fury. "How could you? I trusted you."

Sofía glared at her. "You've always been too soft, your perception tainted the moment you chose a human mate. It wasn't enough that humans destroyed their land and their people. They had to come here and destroy ours. Our people died. *My daughter was taken!* And still you wouldn't close our borders. You thought simply scaring them would make them stop."

"It *was* enough," Madremonte said, and thunder boomed in the throne room. Beside Valentina, Julián drew closer. "My punishments in the human world ceased their destruction."

"Temporarily! Before long, they forgot their fears and went back to their old ways. There's a reason it was called La Violencia in their world!"

Valentina had heard that phrase before, and she didn't think it had anything to do with Papi's experiences when he was a kid. But where?

"Your grand plans of peace between our worlds cost us because humans could not be trusted." Patasola laughed bitterly. "You weren't protecting our land or our people. You were killing us. I had to make you see the truth before it was too late."

"What did you do?" Madremonte demanded.

Sofía looked away, her expression warring between regret and anger. "I lured Marcos into the human world and let humans do what they did best—destroy. I figured maybe then you would finally close the borders. And you did."

The queen howled, clenching her fists. In response, more vines shot out. Valentina stared wide-eyed as they tightened around Sofía, who gasped. She hated the patasola for doing what she did, but two wrongs didn't make a right. Tentatively, she approached her grandmother. The madremonte terrified her in this state, but Valentina couldn't stand by and let her kill Sofía.

"Don't do it," Valentina said softly, placing a hand on her grandmother's arm. "Punish her, put her in the dungeon, but don't end her life."

The queen paused, looking down at Valentina's hand, then at Valentina. She exhaled, unclenching her fists. The vines loosened but didn't let Sofía go. "It seems my granddaughter has more decency than you," she said finally.

"You're wrong, you know," Valentina told Sofía. "Closing the border didn't make you safer; it hurt your own people. It made it so humans forgot you, which is why some of you are disappearing. And humans didn't destroy Marcos. In fact, he was raised by loving people."

Even as she said it, Valentina couldn't shake the feeling that things weren't adding up. If Papi was Madremonte's son, he would've been alive during the Gran Violencia here, which was hundreds of years ago. She knew time worked differently here, but even that seemed like a long time—much longer than her father's forty-two years. And sure, Papi had grown up knowing violence thanks to the cartels and guerrillas, but that was hardly the first violent period in Colombian history.

Suddenly, Valentina knew where she'd heard the term "La Violencia"—in history class, when they learned about a ten-year civil war that took place thirty years before Papi was born.

"How long exactly has the border been closed?" Valentina asked.

"About three hundred and twenty-five years," Madremonte replied. "Sixty-five in human years. Why?"

"How old *are* you?" Julián asked incredulously.

Valentina nudged him to be quiet. She was thinking hard. Papi couldn't be the prince—he wasn't even *alive* when the border closed. But the portrait in the hallway looked just like him and Julián . . .

. . . And Abuelito!

Her family always joked that the three of them had looked identical as little kids. As Julián got older, though, he'd started looking more like Mami. That had to be why the madremonte hadn't seen the resemblance to her son.

But Abuelito . . . he was seventy years old. If the border had been closed for sixty-five years, then that meant her grandfather had been five when the portal sealed.

The exact same age as Marcos when he disappeared.

Everything began clicking into place. The stories Papi told all came from Abuelito. *He* was the one Mami blamed for filling Papi's head with nonsense. *He* was the one who first filled their lives with these enchanting tales.

And then another realization dawned on her. Everyone called her grandfather Abuelito Germán—but his full name was actually *Marcos* Germán Mejía.

"Vale?" Julián asked. "What's wrong?"

"Nothing's wrong," Valentina said, laughing. "It's just, the patasola's right. There's no way we can be Marcos's children."

"What do you mean?" Madremonte frowned. "The locket—"

"We can't be his children because we're his *grandchildren*," Valentina amended quickly. "Our abuelito is your son, not Papi. We're your *great*-grandchildren."

FORTY

Madremonte turned to Rafael. "Call your squad. Release the prisoners and take Sofía here to the dungeon. I will deal with her later. It will be imperative to determine whether she acted alone or if she had accomplices."

El silbón saluted and dragged the struggling patasola away, as loyal as a guard should be, but Valentina couldn't help but notice the sadness that crossed his face.

"I can't believe the traitor was in my own castle this entire time." Madremonte shook her head, looking as if she'd aged centuries in the last few minutes.

"People do strange things when the ones they love are in danger," Valentina said softly. She thought of Julián and Papi, and everything she had faced in the last few days to make sure they were safe.

Madremonte glanced at them, seemingly lost in her own thoughts. "Once we settle the situation with your father, I would love to have you and your grandfather and family here for an honorary banquet. I have too much time to make up for."

Valentina's pulse quickened. "Does that mean the portal will be reopened for good?"

"Yes." Her *great*-grandmother smiled then, and the shadows cleared from her expression. "I can't have found my son and his family just to seal him away. I will have to devise some rules, but yes, the portal between worlds shall remain open."

In a daze, Valentina nodded. She'd be able to come back, to take her time and enjoy Tierra de los Olvidados without worrying about anyone trying to harm them. She'd be able to bring Papi here, to prove to Mami that magic did, in fact, exist. They would come with her abuelitos. She could ride Albetroz through the rivers. She could draw everything!

Once Papi was safe, everything would be just right.

But they needed to get to him quickly.

"It took us three days to get here," she told the queen. "How long is that in the human world?"

Madremonte peered into the portal in her ring. "Just over fourteen hours."

Valentina didn't think she'd ever be able to fully grasp the differences in time between the worlds, but for now, she was just relieved there was hope for Papi. People could survive much longer than fourteen hours without food and water.

"If you'll excuse me," Madremonte said, striding toward the double doors. "I must go get everything I need for the human world. Feel free to wander. This is your home." Her eyes twinkled and she left.

So Valentina did, with a sullen Julián on her heels. While she marveled at everything, he remained scowling. She'd have to talk to him at some point.

Light flooded the castle from the open windows as creatures tore through the hallways, calling orders and making preparations. Soon, Doña Ruth, Grucinda, Armando, and Isabella joined them. While everyone else surrounded Valentina and Julián, Doña Ruth held back. She gave Valentina a sad smile before ambling down the hall. Away from them.

"Wait!" Valentina called, but Grucinda embraced her before she could follow the capybara.

"My dear child," Grucinda cooed. "You succeeded! You've saved us all."

Valentina smiled slightly, her thoughts still on Doña Ruth. "I guess we did."

Grucinda hooked her arm with Valentina's. "When you two stumbled onto this land, I had my suspicions. But I didn't have a chance to investigate further. I never did like that patasola."

At this, Valentina glanced at the brujita. "Why didn't you tell us?"

"Would you have believed me?" Grucinda asked.

"Probably not."

Grucinda chuckled. "In any case, I wasn't completely sure, and then Sofía arrived. But I have been living in that same cottage for too many years, and never have humans crossed over since the border sealed. It was Madremonte's magic, which runs through her blood, that closed it. And it was only Madremonte's magic that could open it again." She winked at them.

Magic. Valentina stared in wonder. She had magic. And maybe that explained a few things. "Right before the earthquake hit, I had a premonition," she told Grucinda. "I felt really sick, kept thinking the earth wasn't happy."

Grucinda beamed. "You have our queen's gifts. Perhaps not to control the rivers and mountains, since you are part human, but I don't doubt for a second you will always feel connected to the earth. And you, too," she added, patting Julián on his head.

He shook his head, rolling his eyes. "I'm not a dog."

"Who's the boring one now?" she whispered to him.

A smile tugged at his lips, but he kept his arms crossed.

If she and her brother were connected to the earth, was that also true for Papi and Abuelito? As far as she knew, they'd never had premonitions like she had. Sure, Papi felt most at ease in nature, diving into lagoons and hiking through the Andes. But many people loved nature. It didn't mean they had *magic.*

"So it's true?" Isabella asked. "You're the queen's great-grandkids?"

Valentina nodded, glancing around. What was taking the madremonte so long? She wanted to be back in the Andes with her father. A nervous energy zapped beneath her skin.

"I still don't believe it," Julián said. "But as long as it gets us home, fine."

Valentina had had enough of his pouting. "Come with me." She pulled him up the stairs, with the duendes on their heels, until they reached the hallway of portraits. She stopped before Marcos's painting. Valentina opened the locket and showed it to her brother, though really, the portrait alone would've been enough proof. "See?"

Julián glanced between the two over and over until his frown smoothed out. He snatched the locket from her, studying it. "Whoa." Then, as an afterthought, he said, "I still don't like her."

"She's going to take us home and save Papi. What more can we ask now?"

He shrugged, but Valentina noticed he wasn't crossing his arms anymore.

"That's amazing," Isabella said.

"Yeah," Armando agreed. "To think we've been in the presence of a princess this entire time and didn't even know it."

A princess.

"Hey, don't forget a prince," Julián said, which was enough to send everyone into uncontrollable laughter, lifting the unease and fear of the last several days.

"Señorita Valentina." She turned, recognizing the voice, though it didn't sound as harsh now. Behind her was el silbón. Where there had been gaping holes in his skull, now two soft hazel eyes watched her.

He bowed. "The queen has requested the presence of both her kin in the Great Hall."

"What happened to your eyes?" Julián said.

Rafael chuckled. "I can do a trick or two. It's all part of my job description."

Valentina and Julián waved goodbye to Armando and Isabella and followed el silbón. As they walked, Valentina studied the guard. He certainly didn't look as imposing now. He still had leathery skin pulled taut over his bones, but without the leering grin, growling voice, or black holes for eyes, he wasn't so scary.

Julián broke the silence. "Do you really kill people and count their bones?"

Valentina bit back a smile. Now, *that* sounded more like her usual annoying brother.

Rafael let out a bark of laughter, which echoed through the hallways. "Where did you hear such an absurd story?"

"Home," Julián mumbled.

Rafael shook his head. "I'm but a simple guard in the queen's service. I serve justice when required. I certainly do not count bones!"

"Then what's in your sack?" Julián asked.

"My prisoners. And sometimes, snacks. Working late nights can get quite hungry."

Snacks! That was so normal. It occurred to Valentina that the legends she'd grown up hearing might be as distorted as the ones about humans here in Tierra de los Olvidados. It was like Mami liked to say: "Memories shift and blur the more time passes."

The Great Hall was even bigger than the throne room—and brighter. Stained glass windows lined the walls, plunging the space into a kaleidoscope of color, and in between hung layers of vines curling and uncurling. On the far end, a fireplace crackled.

And in the center, Grucinda stood speaking with Madremonte, who had changed into a mossy tunic for the journey. The queen was pacing but paused when she heard them enter. "Are you ready?"

"I've been ready since the moment we got here," Valentina said.

"For real," Julián agreed.

Their great-grandmother smiled. "Then let's get you back home."

FORTY-ONE

Madremonte raised her hands, and several vines on the wall parted. Slabs of limestone rumbled, transforming into an archway. Beyond it lay darkness.

Julián stared. "Is that the portal? I thought it was on your ring?"

Their great-grandmother smiled. "My ring powers the portals. While there *is* a portal to your world in the castle, I'm afraid it will leave us far from your father. To reach my grandson faster, we'll want to return to the same spot where you entered Tierra de los Olvidados. This door is my own shortcut to other corners of my land. I believe you'll recognize what's on the other side."

And Valentina did.

Grucinda's cottage was exactly as she remembered. The flowering planters on the wrap-around porch swung in the breeze. The plains gleamed underneath the midday sun. After stepping out of the passageway, the brujita tilted her face up to the sky and then disappeared into her home.

"Come, my dears." The madremonte beckoned them, and Valentina and Julián followed her to the mound of earth that had once been the exit they'd stumbled through. Now their great-grandmother crouched and placed her hands on the earth, her emerald ring glowing bright on her hand. The ring's light pulsed as the madremonte murmured words they couldn't hear, and even though Valentina knew what was coming, she still gaped as the ground groaned and stretched until it formed the yawning opening of the cave.

"I totally want to do magic like that," Julián said.

"When you're older," Madremonte called over her shoulder, "and if your parents allow, I can teach you."

Valentina and Julián exchanged matching grins.

Madremonte turned and faced the plains. Then, in one swift motion, she slashed the air with her hands. Instantly, the earth cracked and parted, and Valentina's heart thundered as she remembered the earthquake.

But there was no rumbling. Valentina watched in awe as water filled the void—a canal!—and soon, a familiar beastly head poked out of the water.

"You're back!" Albetroz shouted, swimming toward them with a giant grin that would have been terrifying if Valentina didn't know any better.

Julián rushed toward the dragon. Valentina ran after him, and together they threw their arms around Albetroz's thick, scaly neck.

"You're okay!" she said. "You escaped the mohán!"

Albetroz slapped his serpent tail on the canal's surface. "Did you doubt me? No creature can beat the great Dragon of the River!"

Madremonte approached, one eyebrow raised. "Is that so?"

Valentina wouldn't have thought it was possible, but Albetroz blushed. "Well, not you, of course, my queen."

The madremonte chuckled and waved Valentina and Julián forward. "Climb aboard."

Julián frowned. "But it's not big enough for him in the tunnel."

"Yeah," Valentina agreed. "It was barely big enough for us last time."

"Ah, but you didn't have your great-grandmother with you then, now did you?" Grucinda had come back out of her house to join them, carrying a bag filled with jars.

"True." Valentina gripped Albetroz's scaly wings and climbed on. Julián went on after, followed by Grucinda and Madremonte.

When they were all mounted, the dragon roared and dove into the newly formed channel, heading straight toward the cave. Valentina shrieked, but this time she didn't close her eyes. The cave's opening widened and stretched, fitting around Albetroz with plenty of room to spare.

It felt like seconds before the boulder came into view at the end of the tunnel. They were approaching too fast. "We're going to crash!" Valentina screamed. Only they didn't. The tunnel glowed bright green and the rock rolled away, allowing them and the water to spill into the ditch behind it.

Julián shook with laughter. "That was awesome! Can we do it again? You know, after Papi's okay?"

One by one, Albetroz raised them out of the ditch and deposited them safely onto the mountain above.

"Gracias," Madremonte murmured.

Early-morning sunlight filtered through the trees, and a few birds tittered and cawed from the tops. Valentina peered through the woods. She had a flashback to the Bosque de Sueños and her heartbeat quickened, but she shook her head. She was in her world now, not some magical, moody forest.

Valentina scanned the earth, trying to find the crack Papi had fallen into among all the debris from the earthquake. Then she heard his voice. "Help! Anyone out there? ¡Ayúdenme!"

"That's him!" Valentina said, running toward her father's voice. Behind her, the others followed. "Papi!"

A beat, and then, "Valentina? Julián?" His voice sounded so weak.

"We're coming!" her brother answered.

Valentina searched around toppled trees, broken branches, and scattered leaves until she found it: a gaping hole in the ground large enough to fit a man. "There." She pointed. "He's down there, but the ground wasn't very stable."

"Say no more." Madremonte knelt, placing open hands on the earth. She closed her eyes, humming softly. A rumbling beneath them seemed to answer her, spreading out through the forest.

Valentina tensed, but Grucinda placed a hand on her arm. "It's fine. She is simply making sure the ground is firm."

Valentina nodded. Julián held her hand. Together, they waited.

When the movement stopped, Madremonte stood. "It's safe."

Valentina didn't need to be told twice. She ran toward the edge, Julián at her heels, and peered into the abyss. There sat her father with his back against the wall of rock and his legs sprawled before him.

"Papi!" she and Julián called down in unison.

Slowly, their father raised his head. Dirt smeared his nose and cheeks and forehead. His canteens lay open on the ledge, as did the cloths that had held their food. Empty. How long since he'd run out of food and water?

But he was alive, and he was staring right at her. "M'ijos?"

"Sí, Papi." Tears wet Valentina's cheeks. "We're here. And we brought help."

"Muy bien." He tried to smile, but it looked more like a grimace. "I'm afraid I can't put much weight on my legs. They got hurt during the fall."

That was when she saw the gashes on his legs.

She reared back on her heels and turned to the others. "He's hurt and he's used up all his food and water." Her voice cracked. "We need to get him up here."

Madremonte strode over. She stared down at Valentina's father for a moment, her hand on her chest. "My grandson," she murmured. But then she turned, her jaw set as she surveyed their surroundings. With a quick nod to herself, she repeated the hand motion she'd used earlier, slashing the air between the space where Papi sat and the ditch where they'd come through the portal.

The earth shook. The crack groaned and widened, as if a giant were pushing out from the inside, until it formed a channel. Water spilled in, filling the space between Papi and the portal and allowing Albetroz to swim through it toward Papi, who cried out in alarm.

"It's okay," Valentina called down to him.

As Albetroz neared, she saw Papi's eyes widen. His fingers reached out tentatively before dropping to his side. He said something, but the swirling of the water snatched his words.

"It's my honor to be of service, my prince," Albetroz boomed. "Care for a lift?"

Papi glanced back toward Valentina and Julián, his features scrunched in confusion.

"He's a friend," she said.

Her father nodded and winced as he stuffed his empty canteens into his mochila. He moved too slow, as if everything were a weight. He was not okay. Was it his legs? Something else? She tried to think through what he'd taught her about dehydration or infection, both real possibilities given the circumstances, but her mind came up blank.

Madremonte knelt between Valentina and Julián. The three watched silently as Albetroz lifted Papi toward them. As he got closer, they reached out simultaneously and heaved him onto solid ground.

"Gracias," Valentina murmured to Albetroz.

"It's been my pleasure serving you, princesita."

Papi groaned as they settled him beside a tree. Valentina threw her arms around him, and though he smelled sour, she held on. Sweat beaded on his face, and he felt too hot.

Madremonte placed a hand on his forehead. "He's feverish."

"From dehydration or the cuts on his legs?" Valentina asked.

"Could be either," Grucinda said. "But I've got just the thing for both."

Julián asked, his voice tiny, "Is he going to be okay?"

Valentina scooted over, putting an arm around Julián's shoulders. "He's going to be fine. Grucinda knows what she's doing."

"Yes, she does," Madremonte said, settling beside them.

Grucinda got to work. She pressed her hands to Papi's chest and murmured, "Hmm-hmm. I see. Yes." She took some powder from a small pouch and dropped it, along with several blades of grass, into a glass jar. Then she turned to Valentina, plucked her tears with a medicine dropper, and sprinkled them in until the mixture resembled a thick paste.

"Aha! Perfect." She ripped Papi's jeans and pressed the goo onto his legs.

Before their eyes, it absorbed the blood on his skin, bubbling over the wounds like hydrogen peroxide—only greener. It shifted from green to purple to a bright pink, and then Papi let out an involuntary sigh.

Valentina gripped Julián's hand, hoping, praying, wishing.

When Grucinda wiped it away, the skin on his legs was clear. No gashes, no scars—nothing to indicate he'd been hurt. She moved his legs gingerly, and when Papi didn't wince in pain, she nodded, satisfied.

Madremonte watched Papi with reverence. "I can't believe this is my grandson." She touched his cheek. Papi blinked up at her, his eyes hazy with confusion, before his lids fluttered closed.

He didn't move. His chest barely rose.

"What's wrong with him?" Julián cried, kneeling beside Papi.

Valentina panicked. This couldn't be happening. Grucinda had magic! The wounds were healed! Maybe he was just exhausted. If they were in Tierra de los Olvidados, she'd give him the water from the rivers.

The water! It was as magical as the land it came from. Would it work here, too?

Valentina slipped off her mochila. With trembling fingers, she rummaged until she found her canteens. She uncapped one and gently lifted it to her father's lips.

"Toma, Papi," she said. "Drink. Fresh water. It'll help you feel better."

Please, please, please let it work. Her father held the liquid in his mouth, then swallowed. The effects were almost instant. He reached up, plucked the canteen from her grasp, and gulped down the rest. When he was done, he licked his lips and opened his eyes, and they shone clear and sharp.

Julián helped Papi up and clung to him.

"That's the best-tasting water I've ever had," Papi said, then stopped as he became aware of the beings surrounding Valentina and Julián. She could see his gaze traveling from Albetroz to Grucinda and Madremonte. "What—?"

Valentina took a deep breath. "Papi, these are Albetroz the dragon, Grucinda la brujita, and Madremonte." She paused, grinning. "Your grandmother."

Papi gaped at them before turning his attention to Valentina. "Is this a dream?"

"It's a long story." Valentina smiled at Grucinda and Madremonte. "The stuff magic's made of."

EPILOGUE

Abuelito paced the living room while everyone in Valentina's home on the finca readied themselves for Madremonte's banquet. "Vamos, everyone!" he called. "What's taking you all so long? I don't want to keep my mamá waiting. You know she'll send el mohán after us!"

Valentina couldn't help but grin as she finished braiding her hair. A couple of weeks had passed since Valentina and Julián had found Papi in the mountains, and so much had changed for her family.

❁

At first, Papi had been sure he was delirious from the fall. But slowly, Valentina and Julián—with some interjections from Madremonte, Grucinda, and Albetroz—had spun a story so fantastical, Papi had realized it could only be true.

Before returning to Tierra de los Olvidados, the queen had promised to open a new portal that connected three places: their finca, their abuelito's place in Bogotá, and her castle. "A shortcut," she said.

Mami had taken more convincing.

After they finally returned to their finca and Valentina and Julián recounted their adventure—this time with Papi's interruptions—their mother had pressed her fists to her hips. "¿Creen que soy boba? I'm not stupid. I couldn't reach you for almost forty hours, and *this* is what you tell me? You were almost killed!"

"But it's true!" Julián insisted.

She threw her hands up and stomped away. Then they heard her scream.

Valentina dashed to the kitchen, only to skid to a stop when she saw Mami wide-eyed with shock. An ornate door carved out of limestone stood in the middle of the far wall, and Valentina knew immediately what it was.

The portal.

When the door opened a few seconds later and Madremonte appeared, Mami all but passed out. But when Madremonte led them all back through the portal to Abuelito's apartment, Mami refused to be left behind.

They found Abuelito sitting at the dining table, enjoying a tinto and bocadillo, when the portal opened. He didn't startle, the way Mami had. Or think he was hallucinating, like Papi had. Instead, as the portal's ornate doorway of vines and leaves opened in the middle of Abuelito's apartment wall, Valentina saw him looking on, curious. Slowly, though, curiosity gave way to wonder and recognition.

He stood suddenly, then, spilling coffee in his haste.

When Valentina and Julián stepped into the small living room, followed by Papi, Mami, and Madremonte, he only had eyes for the queen. The pair stood still, staring at each other, for what seemed like ages, and Valentina could feel the charged tension in the room, could feel both their heartbeats beating in sync and the earth holding its breath.

Finally, Abuelito whispered, "I thought it had all been a dream." And he closed the distance to Madremonte, holding on to her as if afraid she would disappear.

"My son," the queen murmured over and over again.

"Ugh, can we get over the mushy part already?" Julián grumbled, and everyone laughed.

"Cariño," Abuelito called to Abuelita, who'd been in her bedroom, knitting. "I want you to meet someone very important to me."

❁

Now, as Valentina joined Abuelito in the living room, she said, "I still can't believe you're Madremonte's son. You really thought you had imagined it all?"

Abuelito looked behind Valentina for the rest of the family, and when they didn't appear, he sat on the sofa with an impatient huff. Then he nodded. "I suppose I always knew the legends were real, deep down. But when the man who became my papá found me in the streets of Manizales, I was alone and without a history. Whenever I told them that a patasola had brought me here and that I wanted to go home, they just looked at me with pity. They said I was delirious and dehydrated. Off I went to the orphanage, until my papá officially adopted me, and I learned quickly to keep quiet about what I knew. After a while, my memories faded, and I thought I'd imagined them." His gaze had a faraway look.

Valentina placed a hand over his. "But it was all true."

"Yes, well, surviving means blending in." He gave her a rueful smile. "I suppose I started believing what my papá said, but I never stopped feeling as if part of me were missing."

"Are we going or are we going?" Julián demanded.

He'd entered the living room with Abuelita, who looked radiant in her Sunday best. A pearl necklace sat on her neck. Julián, too, had cleaned up nicely, with a pair of khakis and a polo shirt. He'd even brushed his hair.

Valentina rolled her eyes. "Took you long enough."

"You know," Mami said, coming to stand with Papi beside

them, "it would do you well to learn some patience." Mami tugged on her skirt, the only sign that she was nervous. Beside her, in his slacks and button-down shirt, Papi looked completely at ease.

"I'm patient," Valentina grumbled. It was *Julián* who was impatient.

"¿Listos?" Papi asked.

"Ready!" they all cheered as Abuelito opened the portal with his own emerald ring, a gift from his mother.

❀

Sunlight filtered through the stained glass windows of the Great Hall, making rainbows dance above the flowers blooming from the vines on the walls. The room *literally* shook with excitement as fireflies twirled around the swaying blossoms, giving off the appearance of twinkling stars. On the wall above the fireplace, amid orchids and jacarandas, a simple phrase glittered:

WELCOME HOME, MARCOS!

"I can't believe this is real." Papi's voice held a reverence Valentina had never heard before, not even when he slipped into his stories. Everything he'd taught and studied and heard from Abuelito was materialized before him.

"I know, right? It's pretty cool," Valentina said.

Abuelito was surrounded by Grucinda and a group of beings from Tierra de los Olvidados, and he seemed so at ease. There was no hesitation, no fear or awkwardness. It was as if he'd never left at all.

Nearby, Mami stood deep in conversation with Madremonte, who wore a gown of purple hydrangeas and long grass, about plans for getting the earth back in balance. She was telling the queen, who was listening politely, about her work.

"You're doing so much for the land," Madremonte said when Mami paused. "Thank you. For caring and giving. I have some thoughts about what might help to settle the fire burning within the volcanoes, and I promise you my assistance with them."

Mami beamed.

"Where's Julián?" Valentina asked her father.

When he didn't answer, Valentina slipped away. She found her brother racing through the hallways with Armando and Isabella. She smiled, happy to see her brother acting like himself again. All the doors in the corridor were open, casting beams of sunlight over every inch of rock. Tapestries woven from dyed grass hung against the walls and told a new story, of queen and son reunited. Valentina ran her fingers over the likeness of her family.

"Vale!" her brother and the duendes yelled when they saw her.

Valentina giggled, enveloping Armando and Isabella with a hug. "The Elders let you leave the forest alone?"

"We were invited by the madremonte. We couldn't miss your homecoming," Armando said.

A bell chimed throughout the castle. Behind them, someone cleared his throat. Valentina turned, coming face-to-face with el silbón.

"Hola, Don Rafael." Though his clothes still hung from his bony arms and legs, his hair was slicked back instead of disheveled, and his shirt was buttoned to the neck. He even smelled like lavender. "You clean up nice."

"Princesa Valentina." Rafael bowed his head. "It's time for dinner."

Princess. She didn't think she'd ever get used to that. Her life had suddenly become quite enchanted.

She followed el silbón and the duendes back to the Great Hall. Already guests were beginning to sit at a long oak dining table that seemed to go on forever. Valentina took her place between Mami and Julián.

Animals and creatures Valentina had come to know sat across from her and her family. Don Pedro. Doña Ruth. Grucinda. Rafael. Armando and Isabella. The only ones missing were Albetroz, Don Perezoso, Don Babou, and Condor, though Valentina had seen the dragon earlier, when they'd stopped to show Papi Grucinda's cottage.

Valentina caught the capybara's gaze and smiled. Doña Ruth inclined her head. Though Valentina had forgiven her, things were still a little awkward between them. She hoped that with time, they could fall back into the friendship they'd forged in the Bosque de Sueños.

Madremonte sat at the end of the table, and Papi settled between her and Mami. When everyone quieted, the queen rose from her seat. The emerald ring gleamed on her finger.

"Thank you all for coming to this feast, celebrating this momentous occasion. My son, who had been lost, has returned." She paused, lavishing on Abuelito her most adoring gaze. "And with him, we've gained not only an heir, but an entire family." She motioned toward Valentina, Julián, Papi, Mami, and Abuelita before turning back to Abuelito.

"I've dreamed every night of this moment," she continued. "And here you are. The being responsible for your disappearance was apprehended, thanks to your brave granddaughter." She beamed at Valentina.

"Um, I helped too, you know," Julián said, crossing his arms.

Madremonte chuckled.

"Thanks to *both* your grandchildren," she amended. "But enough. Let the feast begin!"

The queen clapped her hands. Almost instantly, several beings who were half human, half alligator came forward dressed in suits of tightly woven grass. They brought all kinds of foods: Roasted duck. Turkey legs. Carne asada. Rice. Red beans. Plantains—both sweet and salty. Empanadas. Chicharrón. Wooden bowls piled high with guavas, mangoes, and grapes. Glass goblets filled to the brim with fruit juices—maracuyá, guanábana, mora. Valentina piled a little of everything on her plate until it could hold no more.

As everyone settled into easy conversation while they ate, Valentina found her fingers itching to draw it all—and it struck her, then, that she didn't have to leave her family for her life to blossom into something extraordinary. She still hoped to attend the Academy of Art in Bogotá one day, but whether or not that happened, she could embrace a life between these two worlds and capture all the magic found in the least likely of places.

She would most certainly be back to Tierra de los Olvidados.

ACKNOWLEDGMENTS

Stories are magical. When I was a child, growing up between two worlds—Colombia and the United States—I spent many summers in my family's finca, Villapaz, which was home to an assortment of fantastical creatures. As my tío would tell it, a brujita lived in the cottage beside the main house. In the copse of bamboo, duendes roamed, and a mighty dragon inhabited the small lake at the edge of the property. My cousin, his daughter, swears to this day that she came face-to-face with a patasola as a child. These stories and those summers spent in Colombia's countryside served to inspire *The Enchanted Life of Valentina Mejía*.

But books do not happen in a vacuum. As the seedling of an idea blossoms into a story and then transforms into a book, there is an entire village of people who help make this happen.

I am eternally grateful to my agent, Deborah Warren, who believed in me and this story from the beginning. You always knew something magical would happen, and it did! To my editor, Sophia Jimenez, thank you for loving Valentina and Julián as much as I do. Your joy and enthusiasm for these characters has meant the world to me. Thank you for your keen editorial feedback and for pushing me to dig deeper. This story is so much better because of you.

Thank you to the rest of the team at Atheneum Books for Young Readers who gave this book a home and made it the best it could be—Justin Chanda, Reka Simonsen, Jeannie Ng, Kaitlyn San Miguel, Tatyana Rosalia, Debra Sfetsios-Conover, and Megan

Gendell. You're all magical! And a huge thank you to illustrator extraordinaire Dana SanMar for your incredible cover.

This book wouldn't have happened without the love and encouragement of my local critique group: Christina Diaz Gonzalez, Alex Flinn, Stephanie Rae, Danielle Joseph, Silvia López, and Gaby Triana. You read some of the earliest drafts and cheered me on through the highs and lows. Thank you; I miss our days at Panera and Starbucks.

To my critique partners, Sarah Lynn Scheerger and Suzi Guina: You've read this story more times than I can count, and I'm forever grateful for your critiques, insights, and support; however, what I cherish most is your friendship. I'm so happy our paths crossed.

To my writer friends whose feedback helped shape this story at different stages—Sonia Hartl, Diana Urban, Laurie Dennison, Juliana Brandt, Zara González Hoang, Reina Luz Alegre, Lacee Little, and Tara Creel—thank you from the bottom of my heart. To Joy McCullough, Amanda Rawson Hill, Cindy Baldwin: thank you for your friendship and expertise in all things publishing and craft. To the members of Las Musas, the Clubhouse, Kidlerati, PitchWars, and SCBWI Florida: thank you for becoming a family and for journeying through this whole writing and publishing thing with me.

To my family—the Peñaloza Arias and Duque Gomez branches—thank you for sharing your love and stories of Colombia with me. A special thanks to my cousins Alejo, Monica, Adela, and Maria Clemencia for your help with my research, and for answering all the questions I had about Colombia, Villapaz, and our legends when my own memories were incomplete.

To Mami: thank you for all those days in the library, which filled my head and heart with stories. And Papi: I miss you. Thank you for always pushing me and filling my childhood with art. I hope you're proud.

To my husband, Jorge: You are my rock. Thank you for always believing in me and telling the world how proud you are. Your support means everything. To my son, Lukas: Thank you for putting up with the countless times I read this story to you aloud. You inspire me every day.

And I'm so grateful to God, whose timing is impeccable, as always.

Finally, to my readers and to the teachers, librarians, and booksellers who will be sharing this story: Thank you for joining me on this enchanted adventure. This is for you.